SEARCHLIGHT ANTHOLOGY

ERIC KERCHER

PAPER AND SWORD, LLC

From the Author

There are days when we all need an escape from a terrible job, a terrible day, or a terrible life.

Join my newsletter and get an escape from the real world, stories, and lore designed to entertain and delight.

You'll also get *Stories from the Deep*, an exclusive, unpublished anthology chock full of extra epilogues, short stories, and lore from the Patmos Sea Fantasy Adventure Series.

Join now at erickercher.com.

Enjoy the book.

-Eric Kercher

Introduction

Astral projection, psychedelic substances, and magical scrolls. What unites all these things?

Not much, if any. But in the collection that follows, they are incorporated into stories of searching. The characters are after something. Sometimes they know what it is, at other times they would be hard pressed to name it if they were asked.

What happens on that search, the journeys that arise after, is part of the mystery and fantasy. How they react tells more about who they are as people, and perhaps reminds us of our own quests for the things that we desire.

Or that desire us.

So come along, take part in these tales of fantastic adventure, and weave your way through them on your own magical journey of life.

-Eric Kercher

1

RED SPHERE OF GLORY

Red dust trickled from the wings of a shimmering pixie, falling on merchants and shoppers alike. Sven knocked the dust off his shoulders and took a few steps before removing his hat.

"Inconsiderate. Where are their manners?" He looked around the busy street as he brushed off the hat, creatures of every shape and size hustling by. "Xavier, where are you?"

"Behind you."

"No need to hide from me. Come on, man. We've got a lot of work to do." Sven narrowed his eyes and sniffed the air as he returned the duster to his head. "I can smell it."

"The only thing I smell is sewage and rotting skunk." Xavier wrinkled his nose and pulled up his mask.

"Ah, but underneath it all lies treasure."

Eying the stall next to him and its copious amounts of skulls, Xavier shifted the backpack towering over his head. It clinked and rattled, drawing a few looks from the passersby and merchants alike.

Sven didn't seem to notice, striding ahead and whistling a sultry tune. Xavier had to run to catch up. "Did I ever tell you about the bistro at the edge of the ravine?"

"Many times."

"Picture it." Sven swung his hands out in an arc, almost knocking over bottles of poisons in the stall next to him. The boar-faced monster manning it barked at him, but Sven kept walking. "The sunset over the horizon, a delectable meal of squid and shrimp toasted over a bed of coals. All paired with the darkest red wine you've ever seen. When I mean red, I mean almost black."

Overhead, a dragon flew by, roaring and sending everyone scattering. Xavier ducked into a stall next to him, but Sven kept walking. He was halfway up the street before Xavier poked his head out and saw that the coast was clear.

Sven was still talking and gesticulating, although the crowded street had emptied. Xavier shrugged his pack up and hurried to catch up.

"--then we all went out for the night." Sven sighed. "I remember it like it was yesterday." Xavier fell in step, matching Sven's large strides.

The market had recovered from the momentary passing of an apex predator, and the street flooded again with bodies pressed up tight against one another. The merchants in the stalls that overflowed, pushing the mass even tighter, had returned to hawking their wares.

"Leg of lamb, eye of newt," called out a particularly grizzled old hag, one eye shut and the other glowing green. Xavier tried to avoid eye contact with her.

"Mystical potions, half off."

"Bring your wood to be transformed! Only four more hours left."

"The finest daggers and blades this side of the Two Bend River." They called out over the voices of the shoppers.

Sven bobbed his head from side to side, finally checking the contents. The stalls stretched on, and he got distracted by the shining blades. Without much warning, he turned right and stopped, forcing Xavier to pull up short.

"Finest blade?" a human snorted, running his hand along a particularly sharp looking straight blade. "I've seen better at my local blacksmith. How much for this? Three coppers?"

"Three coppers!" The fish-headed blade seller snatched the sword away from the man's hand. "Keep your filthy hands off it. It's worth more than forty sovereigns."

"Forty sovereigns! You must be mad." The two haggled back and forth as Xavier tried to catch his breath.

Sven whistled, eying a dagger with a ruby in its hilt. "About the right shade..." he muttered, caressing his chin. "But not big enough." The ruby had a red glow and pulsated with a power of its own.

"You have good taste, friend." The fish-headed merchant slid up to the counter next to them, his business concluded with the other man. He eyed the sword on Sven's hip. "Enchanted by the Witch of the Stillwell Swamp. Can ward its bearer from danger."

"I'm not sure..." Sven agonized over it, turning his head in different directions. "Xavier, what do you think?"

Xavier shook his head. "It won't do for you."

"That's what I was thinking, too."

The eyes of the fish-man opened wide.

"Surely you can reconsider? I sense great power in you, and this dagger will do more than cut up your bread." He picked it up. "Go ahead, touch it. Feel how light it is, and how well balanced."

He handed it to Sven, perched on his fin-like hand. Sven hesitated, then picked it up. "It is light. Sturdy too. I hadn't expected that." He took a few test cuts in the air, then flipped it in the air and caught it. "Handles nicely."

"You've always hated knives."

"You're right, you're right." Sven put it back, careful not to touch the edge. "I wouldn't see much use in it, anyway."

"Only four hundred sovereigns," the merchant said. "A special price for you, all considering the trouble I had to go through to get it. The Witch refused to take it by spell. I had to travel to her house myself."

"Do I have enough?" Sven asked, picking it back up.

"Sven."

"Oh, I know. Don't look at me like that. I can't help myself. It looks right." He wilted under Xavier's gaze. Xavier took it out of his hand and put it back.

"It isn't what we came for."

"Three hundred," the merchant blurted out, eyes darting between them. "And I'll sharpen it. I can't go any less."

Xavier shook his head and turned Sven back to the street.

"Two-fifty!" the merchant called back to them, but it was no use. They rejoined the throng, slipping behind a pair of fighters dressed in heavy leathers. In a few more moments, they were gone.

"So close on that one, I almost thought we had it."

"Yes." The fighters split the crowd, making it easier for them to travel. Xavier tried to look past them. He didn't have the height to look over them like Sven could.

"It was nearly the right color."

"Wrong material though."

Sven sighed. "I'm glad you came with me. I don't know where I'd be without you."

"Lost."

Bellowing with laughter, Sven leaned over and slapped his thigh.

Xavier shifted the backpack again. "May I suggest we continue our search?"

"Yes, yes. Off we go." He wiped the sides of his eyes, wet with laughter, and they continued on.

Stall after stall, the market stretched on. The morning sun turned to afternoon, and then peaked and started its journey back to the horizon. Goods of all kinds were on display.

Exotic animals in their enchanted cages, lumps of ore that dwarfs and craftsman squabbled over, weapons and shields and armor galore.

"Shall we stop for a meal?" Xavier suggested as they left a promising spice merchant.

"Yes, my mouth is watering." Sven rubbed his hands together in glee. Xavier's pack had grown a few bottles heavier. "Do you have it?"

He slung the backpack down and opened the flap. After a few more moments of rustling and rearranging, Xavier produced a block of cheese wrapped in oilcloth, a hunk of ham, and a crusty loaf of bread.

Sven juggled the ham and cheese as they walked over to a square with a fountain in the middle. Other buyers lined up on the edge of the green water, eating their own food. Sven eyed some sort of meat-on-a-stick a few giants were eating on the other side of the unicorn statue spewing the green liquid.

"Do you think we'll find it?" Xavier asked, slicing off a piece of each food and handing it to Sven.

"Of course." Sven's eyebrows wrinkled. "I *have* to have it, Xavier. You know how important this is to me."

"I know." He grimaced. "But how long should we look for it?"

"I'll stay here all week if I have to."

"I know." Xavier sighed. "Like all the other trips, I guess that means we'll need some lodging tonight, then." He looked back into the market, tucked in between the squat, yellow sandstone buildings.

The castle rose above it all in the background, flags fluttering in the breeze. Sven reached over and patted Xavier on the leg. "Stick with me. I know you want to be at home."

Xavier bit off his layered food and chewed thoughtfully. He looked back down at his stack of foods with a hint of a smile. "It's good."

"Do you think those cost much?" Sven asked, nodding to the meat on a stick. "They look tasty."

"I'd be more concerned about what they are." The meat was lumpy, and Xavier thought he spied eyes as the giant took a bite. He shuddered. "We'd better be on our way."

"Perhaps a bite of something sweet?" Sven had devoured his food, licking his fingers of the last crumbs and fat.

"I'll defer to you." Xavier cut him another, and barely had time to finish his own before Sven had bolted to a short, hunchbacked lady pushing a cart piled with sweets.

"We'll take two, no four, of your best."

"My what?" She leaned in, cupping her ear.

"Four of your best," Sven bellowed, cupping his hands around his mouth. She startled back at the noise.

"My, my!" She smoothed out her dress. "I heard that part. Do you want sweet breads or honey buns?" she cackled.

Sven drew back, tapping his chin. He scratched the back of his head, then shrugged. Xavier had caught up at this point, backpack back in order and balanced once again.

"Honey buns," he said.

"Two of each then," Sven said, motioning Xavier forward.

"Two bits each." She scooped up his choices with gnarled hands, but held them close to her chest until Xavier had produced the coins. The exchange was made, and Sven took the bulk of the catch.

Munching on his bun, Sven wandered down another street of the market. The honey clumped and stuck to Sven's thick fingers. One bun disappeared, then the sweet bread after.

"Mmm..."

"Don't even think about it." Xavier said, wrapping up his and tucking them into his pocket.

"We could go back and get some more?" His eyes pleaded with Xavier.

"Remember what we came for." The bustle and chaos of the market enveloped them again, and they kept walking.

"Eye on the prize, eh?" Sven drew himself up. "You're right." His eyes flashed, and he surveyed the stalls with renewed energy.

The sun sank down. Up and down they went. Into and out of stalls. The hard bargaining of the day had taken away the gusto of all but the best merchants. No longer did they stand at the entrance to their stalls and shout out the benefits of their goods.

Now, with the sun nearly to the horizon, they were resigned to their stools and blankets, or the hard ground.

And still Sven stalked through the stalls, Xavier close behind. The crowd had thinned, giving them space to walk side by side.

"Shall we retire for the night?" Xavier asked. He was shifting the backpack more often.

"Not yet. The day is still young." Sven waved away a pixie who was trying to attract them to its crocodile leather store. "Begone with you." He swatted at it.

The small creature said something rude in a high-pitched voice, then shook its tiny little fist before moving to the next one. It didn't seem to affect Sven, who kept peering into the stalls.

"Not so young anymore," Xavier said. Merchants closed down around them, packing up their wares or drawing down flaps of their tents. The sun was leaving, and so were they.

A different sort of clientèle was streaming into the marketplace, with a different set of tastes. The marketplace seemed to change all at once as soon as the sun started casting a brilliant spray of colors into a sunset.

Dark shapes slinked in through the alleys and back roads. Xavier was the first to notice, and he pulled tighter on the straps of the backpack and patted his hip.

"It would be a good time to go find a place to sleep," he said. The streets that had emptied were now starting to fill up. Merchants carrying...darker wares were setting up shop. Enchanted skulls popped up on rune covered blankets, potions replaced by poisons, and even the food had turned dark.

"I smell something. Up ahead." Sven pushed on.

"I really think we should go..."

"Only a few more, and then we'll go. I promise." Sven held up his large little finger. Xavier sighed and entwined his.

"I don't know why you still do this. We haven't been children for a while."

"Promises kept, promises made."

"Keep it secret, never fade," Xavier grumbled. Sven nodded, then turned back down the street. Even though half the stalls were closed, there were more that had appeared out of nowhere.

Xavier looked back over his shoulder as they passed another stall. He tripped and fell, but caught himself with his hands. The backpack clanked and rattled.

One of the flagstones was poking up above the rest in the street. "Watch out for that," Sven said cheerfully. Grunts and the sounds of squabbling drifted up the street.

"I think I've seen that before. Have we come this way already?"

"Don't know." Sven helped him up.

"We have, I recognize this. We've been going in circles, haven't we?"

"You've passed this way before." The crackling voice crawled out of a stall next to them. Crushed between two larger black tents, they had missed it the first time they went by.

A squat, fat goblin crouched in the shadows, a copper earing dangling from his left pointed ear. "You've been stopped for a reason." It spread a shriveled hand across its blanket. "Stop and see the goods I offer."

Xavier and Sven backed up as a giant stomped by, rattling their bones. "I don't have a good feeling about this," Xavier whispered.

"What is that?" Sven was mesmerized by something.

"Ah, you have an eye for the mystical." The hand waved him closer. "A rare and exotic find." The sounds amplified as a group of orcs rounded the corner.

"I think…" Sven took a step closer.

"If this doesn't interest you, then I have others like it." The goblin patted the dark red, and shiny, object. There were other things with it. A pile of small bones, a roll of cloth, small baubles.

Eyes wide, Sven stepped across the street and into the goblin's stall. "Where did you find this?" He reached out with a tentative hand.

"Eh?" The goblin leaned in closer. The orcs were causing a ruckus, drowning out everything around them. Xavier hurried to catch up, stepping out of their way.

"I said where did you find this?" Sven bellowed. An orc turned his head at the intrusion.

"Far to the south," the goblin said. A hand reached out and pushed Sven aside. "Over the--"

"Pretty," an orc grunted, picking the red sphere. It held it up above its head in the dying light. "Give it to me."

The goblin's eyes narrowed. "For the right price," it said, only a touch of annoyance in its overly polite tone.

Sven's mouth gaped open as he stared up. Xavier looked nervously, counting the orcs. Seven in the group, now attracted to the stall.

They surrounded them.

"Puny goblin." The orc leaned in and stepped closer. Horns circled around its head. "I'll smash your guts and eat out your brain. Give me what I want."

"Oy! I saw that first. It's mine." Sven stared up at the orc, pointing a finger at the sphere.

"That's it?" Xavier asked, glancing around them.

"Has to be. And I saw it first." The orc's attention had been captured by the interruption, and it turned a beady set of eyes on Sven.

"Puny human. Stay out of this, or I smash you, too." The voice thundered. Xavier hated to think what it sounded like when the orc yelled. The other 'orcs perked up. Their leather armor creaked.

Xavier eased something out of his cloak, eyes glancing around them. "Perhaps we look elsewhere?"

"Other puny human right," another orc said, cracking its knuckles. "Go away."

"We could let them stay," offered another, caressing its axe. "Test their mettle."

"No fighting in the market," the goblin said, and licked its lips. Somehow it had shrunk down even smaller. "You know the rules," it managed to squeak out.

The first orc growled, but Sven turned back to the goblin. "How much?"

"Thirty pieces of gold," the goblin said, gaze shifting back and forth between them.

"You give it to me for free," the orc said, raising a fist. It still held the sphere in the other hand. "Or maybe I take everything else too."

"I can't do that," the goblin said.

"I'll pay the gold," Sven said. He reached out his hand to Xavier, who was otherwise preoccupied. "Xavier, the purse."

"I don't think..."

"Come now," Sven said. "Merchant, do we have a deal?" The orcs reeked of blood and smoke, it came off them in waves.

"Counteroffer?" the goblin said, almost imperceptibly.

"You leave now," the orc said, turning to Sven. "And you live."

Xavier already knew the answer, but there was nothing around them that would help. The guards that mingled with the crowd earlier were nowhere to be seen, and the street had emptied for some reason.

Even the stalls had closed up. Xavier suspected the goblin would have done the same if the option was available to him.

"I'll have to take his offer, unless you can beat it," the goblin said. The orc raised his hand, and the goblin cowered. "The rules!"

Slowly, the enormous fist lowered. The anger burned off the pale skin, rising up into the night. "Thirty-one gold."

Relief flooded across the wrinkled goblin's face, and the hands it threw up to protect itself came down. It looked back to Sven.

"Thirty-two."

"Sven," Xavier said.

Sven held up a hand. "You know I need this."

Xavier cleared his throat and leaned down, shifting his center of gravity lower and rising to the balls of his feet.

"Thirty-five," the orc said. The grunts were quieter now, and grips tightened on handles of weapons. The goblin's eyes shifted between the two bidders.

"Forty," Sven growled, blissfully unaware of the group surrounding him. They pressed tighter to the stall, cutting off all avenues of escape.

The head orc's eyes tightened. "Fifty." Froth flew from its lips, hand still gripping the sphere.

Clearing his throat again, Xavier tried to get Sven's attention, but it was in vain.

"I'll match it, plus five."

"Give up, human. Or else you'll regret it."

"You give it up. We found it first," Sven said, puffing up his chest. Xavier wanted to crawl away to survive another day.

"It's mine." The orc looked down at his hand, then its eyes opened wide. "Where did it go?"

"Right here, safe and sound," the goblin said. The sphere was back on the blanket, shining among the other worn and shabby items in comparison. "Fifty-five is the high offer."

The orc reached out to take it again, but Sven said something first. "It isn't yours. Leave it be."

"Fifty-six." The orc kept reaching. But then Sven's hand was on the hilt of his sword. A glimmer of moonlight reflected off the inch of bared steel.

"Sixty." Their eyes met, fire exchanged between them. The orc stopped reaching.

"Boss," one of the orcs said. "We don't have that much." The street was quiet, the sounds of the market distant. Gone were the loud merchants hawking their wares and the sounds of busy shoppers.

Glancing back to the goblin, who offered a shrug, the orc withdrew its massive arm. "Well then, looks like you got it." Cold fire raged in its eyes. "Didn't really want it, anyway."

Sven's sword clicked back into place, and he nodded. "Very good. Xavier, the money, if you please?"

Keeping an eye on the orcs, Xavier reached into his shirt and counted out the right amount.

The head orc turned back, sauntering back to its companions. It glanced down at Xavier, then shouldered by him.

Sven wasn't paying attention anymore, and had turned his attention back to the sphere. His eyes glowed as they rested upon it.

"You won't be leaving with it, though." The words pricked upon Sven, who turned.

The orcs were lined up in the street, weapons drawn, the head orc in front. In its hands was a massive double headed battle axe, chipped in places and well worn.

Other weapons adorned the other orcs. Wickedly curved swords, axes, and a deadly-looking mace.

The goblin squeaked, and then was gone with all its wares. It left the sphere, lonely on the cold ground.

"No way out," Xavier said.

"I see that." Behind them was a brick wall, a back of a building of some sort. "Gentlemen," Sven continued, in a louder voice, "this is your chance to walk away unharmed. I suggest you take it."

The orcs looked to him, then back to each other, and burst out laughing. The leader, however, did not.

"I'm going to devour your heart and feed your brains to my warg." The orc started forward, a hulking beast.

"Well then," Sven said. "You had your chance."

Xavier shrugged off the backpack and took up his place beside Sven, and sighed. "Almost made it out without incident."

The orc lifted its axe and charged, screaming in rage. "Save it!" Sven called out.

Xavier jumped and plucked the sphere off the ground, rolling over the rough flagstones.

The axe came down.

Sven stepped to the side at the last minute, moving faster than his weight would suggest. "Leave off."

Instead of backing down, the orc elbowed him. Sven tried to avoid it, but got caught in the chin and knocked back.

After staggering a few steps back, Sven recovered. A hand went up to his nose and came away bloody.

The orc smiled. "First blood. Kill them." The other orcs hooted and grunted in pleasure, then charged in.

Sven set his jaw and wiped the blood off on his pants. The sword was out in an instant, flashing. Up and to the right he swung, and the edge dragged along the lead orc.

Now it was his turn to back up and raise his axe in defense. The other orcs were closing in on both of the humans, but the leader raised a hand.

"This one is mine," it thundered. Wetness spread from under its leather breastplate, a gash running up the front where Sven had struck.

As one of the other orcs turned to Xavier, two more holding back to prevent his escape.

Wild eyes flashed, and teeth bared. Xavier slipped the sphere into his pocket, careful to pad it to keep it safe.

Next to him, Sven attacked. "You'll regret this," he snarled. "I could be back at home by now, enjoying my treasure." The sword flashed, and sparks flew as the orc struck it away with his axe.

"Rarghh," the orc cried, pushing off the sword and trying to strike Sven with the butt of his axe.

Sidestepping, Sven avoided the blow and another attack that followed it. The orc was faster than he expected, and didn't see the knee that drove into his stomach.

The air left his body, and stars swam in his vision. Sven ducked, narrowly avoiding the axe, and backed up a few steps.

His back bumped into the brick wall.

The orc pulled back his axe and swung. Sven dove left. The axe smashed into the wall. Bits of brick and dust rained down on him and invaded his nose.

His sword clattered to the ground, but there was no time to get it. Scrambling and cutting up his hands and knees, Sven rushed out of the way.

The axe followed him, chewing up the flagstones. Air rushed on the back of his legs, and he could barely keep ahead of the orc.

Xavier was up ahead, fending off orc attacks with his daggers. He moved like water, dodging and weaving as if the orcs were standing still.

But that was all Sven had time to notice before he was able to get to his feet and glance behind him.

Horns was swinging his axe from behind him. It whistled through the air, and Sven barely had time to jump out of the way before it made a crater in the ground. Rock fragments cut and stung his hands and face.

On the ground, his sword glinted in the moonlight. The orc, swung off balance from the powerful blow, had recovered and was yanking on the handle. Sven seized the opportunity and rushed in, smashing Horns in the face with an elbow.

At first Sven wondered if he had missed and hit the wall instead. The orc's face was solid, and didn't even look like he had touched it.

His elbow, on the other hand, had felt it. Now it was throbbing, and Horns had broken his axe free.

"That all you got?" Horns said, but Sven pushed him out of the way, or tried to. It ended up knocking him off balance, and he staggered forward before the orc could turn and kill him.

That was all he needed.

Sven leaned into the fall he felt coming and redirected it. Air parted behind him as the axe missed where he had just been.

He tucked his shoulder, felt the impact of the ground and another sharp pain, and rolled.

Up he came, hand closed around the slick grip of the blade. He spun around, swinging, and knocked the next attack away.

His heart was beating in his ears, drowning out the sounds of the battle and rushing blood through his body.

Horns wasn't relenting, and pounded away. Blow after blow Sven knocked them aside, searching for an opening. He gave ground, and Horns took it.

One step back, then another, he pushed forward with a counterattack. The orc let his attack hit, cutting into his breastplate again. It didn't stop, and it didn't even seem fazed. Spittle dripped from its mouth as it roared in anger.

"Whew." Sven chopped away, "Someone needs to freshen his breath."

Curses from an orcish tongue flew his way, and Horns charged. Sven cut into his shoulder, but couldn't move out of the way in time.

Together they crashed into the tent poles of the stall behind them. Canvas fell down and covered them. Sven scrambled to pull it off, while landing a few hits of his own on the orc, and received just as many in return.

Finally, he rolled free, thrashing the last clinging bits of leather away, sword still firmly in his hand. He looked up just in time to see an orc charging Xavier.

Two orcs were down, but another was keeping Xavier distracted from the front. "Behind you," Sven said, and took off at a dead sprint.

He ignored the fire that was burning in his lungs. The orc raised a jagged scimitar over its head. The other had Xavier pinned down, axe crushing Xavier's dagger. He was barely holding it off.

Xavier was going to die if he didn't do anything.

And he would be responsible.

All the cajoling and needling, the semi-forced journey had been his idea. Xavier, like usual, had been reticent, but Sven needed him. Sven knew that Xavier knew that, and played it to his advantage.

Sven sprinted forward to help, but something caught his foot. The something gripped hard. Very hard. It yanked, and he fell to the ground. Even though he caught himself in time, it wasn't fast enough to stop him from hitting his head on the ground.

Stars swam in his vision and his eyes stung. He was being pulled back, scraping against the rough stone.

Ignoring the pain, Sven brought up his other foot and mustered all the force he could. When he was ready, he glanced back and aimed, sending his kick smashing into the orc's face.

He hoped it got something soft, because he felt a nice healthy crunch beneath his heel. Glad he brought the heavy boots, Sven applied the same technique to the fingers holding his foot.

One by one they fell. At last the grip was broken, and Sven surged forward like a cork coming out of the water.

Xavier had managed to fend off his attackers, and was dealing with the remaining two orcs. Blood was running down his side, but his gray eyes were hard and painless.

Sven spit out a trail of blood and turned to face his foe.

It was barely in time, because the orc was swinging at him. Sven ducked, but not fast enough, and the side of the axe clipped his head.

He brought his sword up in a counterattack, but the orc shrugged it off and stepped in closer. It hit him in the stomach with the butt of its axe, then shoved him back.

Nearly toppling over, Sven struggled to keep on his feet. The ground was too uneven and forced him backwards with a sickening out of control feeling.

He was halfway across the street before he caught himself. Sven lurched back up, just in time to parry another strike from Horns. Another counterattack, and another cut that didn't faze the orc.

Sweat was stinging his eyes, dripping down from his forehead. The orc's skin was thick. It was going to take more than a few slashes to get through it.

And Horns wasn't helping either. Even with one eye swelling shut from Sven's kick, the orc was still terribly strong, and faster than it should be.

Metal scraped on metal as Sven parried the attacks that never seemed to stop. Once again, he was pushed back, once again the orc was gaining the upper hand.

Then, out of the corner of his eye, Sven caught a glimpse of the flagstone just to the left and behind Horns.

After deflecting another blow, Sven shifted his weight to his left foot and gathered all the strength he had remaining.

He fueled it with anger. Anger at having his prize taken from him, anger at almost losing his life, anger at his own foolishness.

A quick crouch, then Sven exploded forward. His shoulder caught the orc in the stomach, knocking it back a step. Sven attacked again and again, slashing and cutting as fast as he could.

His blade became a whirl, and at first the orc was pushed back. Cuts and slashes landed, but Horns wasn't going to give up either.

One or two steps short of the flagstone, the orc retreated into the defensive and stopped moving back.

Sven desperately kept up the attack, almost all his energy gone. He reached deeper, screaming out in rage and anger. "I will not be denied!"

And then Xavier was at his side. Sven fell into their old ways, almost merging their attacks. Xavier struck like lightning, and the two of them overwhelmed Horn's defenses.

The orc fell back one step, then one more, holding up his axe to try to stop them.

'Its heel caught the flagstone, then it toppled back.

Sven stepped forward, raised his sword over his head, and brought it down on the orc's exposed neck.

The blade bit.

The orc's life ended.

Panting, muscles quivering and shaking, Sven looked up.

The other orcs were dead. Xavier had a few cuts and scrapes, but didn't look too much worse for wear.

"Are you hurt?"

"Not as much as they are," Xavier said. He slipped a hand into his pocket and produced the red sphere.

Sven sighed and slunk to his knees. With a shaking hand he took the sphere.

He held his prize aloft in the moonlight, admiring the red flesh. It was tender, and succulent, and filled with promise.

Xavier wiped his knives off on his trousers and shook his head. "All that for a tomato."

2

THE SMELL OF COFFEE

The coffee was thick and black, still steaming from the brew. I wish I hadn't bought it, it was too strong for me and I needed less focus for the task at hand.

Once more I pushed away all thoughts and let myself free and slipped back into that dreaming state that kept me alive.

Out over the roofs I soared, to the cosmos, through all space and time, until my body responded and I returned to where I was.

Then, with great difficulty, I rose up like a feather and started the journey. I neither turned left nor right, but somehow wound through the earth and over the hills.

Out into that vast desert, where the cactus fails to grow. A desolate place of death and destruction, that only is touched by life when it rains.

And into the tunnel I flew until I last reached the door.

To be polite, I knocked, no sound made from my hand. It opened to me, revealing the dark form and scaled from head to toe.

"You're late."

"Had to stop by and gets something for myself."

The creature grumbled and stepped aside, and my form drifted in.

"Coffee?" it asked.

"No thank you." I squirmed in my semi-real form and took up a seat hovering a few inches across the table.

It didn't have enough room to accommodate my legs, so I tucked them behind myself on the cushion.

Simon, the creatures, took up a boiling pot and poured it over some green liquid. It turned the color of dust and smelled of burnt hair, and then he took a sip.

"Still good. So, you've come to ask my help."

"Yes, I have. Once again I find myself in an....awkward predicament." I shifted my not eyes elsewhere. It wasn't like seeing, more like feeling, but the effect was the same on whoever I was talking to, so it was always polite to maintain an air of decorum.

"Hmm." He grunted, then set down his cup and flopped onto the cushion beside me. "What can I do for you?"

"You could make it disappear, like last time."

"You know that won't work."

I sighed. "I know, but surely there's something you can do?"

"Yes, many things." He gestured around him, to the earth. "I can make things die, and I can make them grow. But that isn't the solution you seek, is it?"

"No." I kicked my leg, passing through the cushion below me.

"Have you tried confronting this accuser in public, take him to task?"

I shook my head furiously, locks of hair flying. "No, that won't work. You know I would die of embarrassment before I ever could do that."

"I know you not well enough yet." He sipped again. "I know what I can do."

"What is it?" This was what I was waiting for, a solution that might mean something. That would make my little problem go away.

"You can leave me alone," he growled. "I'm busy here and you keep interrupting my sleep."

"Darian, you've been sleeping for years. How do you need more of it?"

"Don't you dare tell me what I need." He passed a scaling hand across his eyes. "I apologize, I haven't had enough to eat lately and it makes me angry."

"This might be something that we both can agree on then. Tell you what, I'll keep you supplied with the best bread I can make and you give me some help."

His face brightened, the corners of his lizard lips curling into a smile. A frightening smile that revealed those long teeth.

I was glad he couldn't touch me. Then it hit me. What was I even offering? How would I get fresh bread all the way out here?

"Done." he said, before I could take it back. I pursed my lips.

But it was too late. He scrambled into a sitting position, crossed his legs, then propped his arms on them.

Eyes closed, he went motionless. A sphere of light rose from his back, expanding and contorting into a circle, then an annulus. It settled on his head, wreathing it like a halo.

Something went through me, other than my emotions. Maybe this wasn't a bad deal after all. I could figure out a little logistics, after all.

A weird sound issued from his throat, and it reverberated through the packed earth tunnel. It had to be in some language I wasn't familiar with.

Then, all of a sudden it stopped, his eyes snapped forward, and he flicked me straight between the eyes.

It was like my mind was attached to a massive fishing rod and something pulled. I went flying back, swishing through the universe and narrowly avoiding all the planets, until I slammed back into my body.

Pain, everywhere. I groaned and opened my eyes, finding myself back in my armchair, TV still going, and my coffee cold beside me on the table.

I couldn't move my body, and started to panic, but the pain subsided and the paralysis receded. My fingers twitched, and I could wiggle my toes.

My mouth, dry as cotton, started to work again, flooding with saliva, and I opened it carefully.

"What did he do to me?" I wondered out loud, then coughed. How long had I been gone? The coffee was ice cold, but I drank it anyway, thankful to have something in my belly.

That was stupid. Again, I hit myself. What was I thinking?

Then I shivered, realizing that it was worth it, whatever had happened. I started and ran to the mirror, feet and legs working properly enough to hobble.

Anxiously I examined myself. Still had all my parts. Still looked the same. I touched my body just to make sure. It was real.

So then what had just happened to me? I thought about going back, asking him, but I was too hungry to think about doing it now, and too tired.

So I went to the kitchen instead, yanked open the fridge and rummaged around.

Thoughts overtook me, and the meal was made as if by magic. Wandering, wondering. Had I done the right thing?

I glanced up at the clock, halfway through my peanut butter and jelly sandwich.

My eyes bulged. Dropping everything, I hurried to the door.

My keys weren't there, and a momentary panic attack over-took me. What had I done with them?

Frantic searching, then finally in the bedroom I clutched the hard pearls of metal. I rushed out, locking the door behind me, and practically sprinted.

Sally was going to be so mad at me. I'd have to think of something to explain why I was so late. A train-wreck? No. Meteor hit my house? Wouldn't work.

I settled on traffic, blazing through the traffic light that had blazed amber at me.

The open sign was already flipped when I got there. I grimaced.

Weight hung over me as I turned the corner and parked. I settled on the back door.

I wrinkled my nose at the trash smell that filled the alleyway, overcoming the fresh scents of grass and tree pollen. The collector still hadn't come, and the dumpster almost overflowed with trash and flies swarming around it.

Gingerly, I turned the cold knob, praying that I wouldn't be found out. The door squeaked halfway, and I froze.

I needed to get that fixed. But the coast was clear, the stacks of ingredients and paperwork around my half desk looming up like sentinels. Her sentinels.

Pulling the door behind me, I softly shut it with barely the tiniest of clicks.

"You're late." I winced and turned.

Arms crossed, Sally stood tapping her foot with a frown. Traffic, remember the traffic.

"I... I got caught by sharks," I stammered. Sharks? I cursed my mouth inwardly and cringed.

The smallest of twitches appeared at the corner of her mouth. An eyebrow rose almost to her dark brown hairline. "Sharks? In the middle of Arizona?"

"Big ones." I nodded solemnly.

She said something in a different language. "Get to work, we have customers." I registered the bell. "You're supposed to be in charge of the place, not me."

"I'll do better." I swung my purse onto my desk, scattering a pile of invoices. Sally disappeared into the kitchen, and I caught my breath.

Even that small taking to task left me breathless. I don't know why, she wasn't yelling at me, but the firm, disappointed voice cut me to the bone.

She was right, I should be better. But the scones couldn't wait, so I followed.

Apron on, hair pulled back and covered, I slipped into the familiar routine of the morning, if a bit later than normal.

The kitchen was clean and bright, done over by Sally to sparkling perfection. That made me wince again, but I was thankful for her.

Fresh bread lay in trays, wafting its delicious smells through the warm room. Through the doorway I heard the sounds of commerce, glad for the customers that came.

They talked and laughed, exchanged money for baked goods, and wore smiles that I glimpsed through the round window of the door.

I smiled, hitched up my sleeves, and started humming. It was a lovely tune I remembered from my youth, light and airy, and I set to work.

Flour flew, tickling my nose. Eggs cracked, milk splattered into the big mixer. With a wink I added a bit of love and magic, stirring it in with the rest.

The work caught me, pulled me up and whisked me away. I sighed with pleasure to think of all that would enjoy these blueberry scones, and before I knew it, they were in the oven and browning.

I set a timer, washed my hands and doffed my hair net.

Sally manned the register, ringing up clients. "There you are Mr. Write." She handed him the brown bag and steaming cup of tea.

"Thank you, my dear, you're the highlight of my morning." He touched his hat before accepting them with a pleasant smile. "And can I say how lovely you look?"

"You may not. Move along." Sally was already helping the next customer.

I reached out and patted his shoulder. "Keep at it, she'll thaw out soon."

"You give an old man hope." With a wrinkled hand he patted mine, then turned and went.

"Give me a hand." Sally waved me over, and I was swept up in helping customers and old friends.

Some I knew their selection by heart, others tried to surprise me. With a smile I doled out our treasures of yeast and flour. Light fluffy croissants, hard shelled French breads with spongy interiors, and cookies soft and still warm.

The bell dinged. My eyes glanced over, then my smile froze on my face. The line shortened as the man grew close.

Why did he have to be so tall? It was worse that way. One by one the line advanced, and I helped with robotic movements.

But the time would come, and I dreaded it. Finally, he was at the front.

"Peter, good morning." Was my voice higher than normal?

"One cookie, chocolate chip," he said.

"Of course. Anything else?" I tried to say with as much decorum as I could muster.

"That's a pie."

I looked down. My traitorous hands were holding the apple pie. "I know. Just checking to see if it was still firm." My stomach rumbled. I must not have had enough to eat.

"Break time," Sally said. I whipped my head over, but she was already gone, her apron floating to the floor. Curse her!

"On second thought, I'll take some tea also." Oh no. Three more minutes. "Black please." Make that four.

"To go?" I asked, peering around his broad shoulders. There was no one else. A twinge tweaked me in my belly, and I frowned. There was no one else in line.

"For here." His blue eyes bored into mine.

"Of course." I couldn't keep the exasperation from my voice.

"You haven't answered my proposition," he said. I turned back to get the hot water and tea bag. "Oh?"

The top tore easily with a satisfying rip. I unwound the string and dropped it into a beautiful blue teacup.

The hot water steamed as I poured, puffs of it rising to warm my face. "I deserve an answer." I couldn't give him an answer.

My stomach growled again, a clear warning. My insides jiggled and spun. What was going on?

I flipped the black tea hourglass, and the sand started dropping in 'its tan line. "Any cream with your tea?" I asked, not turning around. I was starting to get concerned.

"No. But I do want an answer."

I turned. "Your tea will be ready in a few minutes, would you like to wait?" I took his money, slamming down on the register, and gave him his change.

Then, before I could stop it, I let out a small fart.

All the blood drained out of my face. Did he hear it?

"I'll wait here."

"We have an open chair right over there." I pointed to it. "I'll bring your tea."

He narrowed his eyes. "Are you okay?"

Another one was coming. I tried to hold it in, but it slipped out with a squeak.

My eyes shot to my watch, conveniently away from his boring gaze. She still had ten minutes left in her break.

And my body was feeling horrible. What did I eat? It smelled like rotten eggs now, and I farted again.

I squeezed my cheeks together, but it happened again. Peter was about to say something, mouth opened, when a timer rang in the kitchen.

"My scones!" I spun, grateful for the excuse to run into the kitchen. As soon as the doors swung shut behind me relief flowed through my body, and I stopped farting.

The scones were done, just a tad too brown, and I pulled them out to cool.

"Sarah, you can't hide from me forever." Peter's voice drifted in through the still swinging door. "I need your answer."

I took a moment, leaning back against the fridge. Then, I remembered.

The tea!

My desire to serve overcame my fear and anxiety, and I steeled myself and went back in just as the last grains of sand slipped down.

But my stomach spun in knots as soon as I came through the door, and the flatulence came back, worse this time.

My ears and cheeks were burning as I handed the cup. "Will that be all?"

"Think about it. I'll be back tomorrow." His nose wrinkled. "What is that smell?"

"Spoiled eggs," I said, reacting without thinking. "We had a bad batch come in from the farm this morning." Thankfully, they had all been silent. I was mortified. Peter gave me a sidelong look, filled with suspicion, and then thankfully took his tea and went.

He watched me from the chair I offered earlier.

My body continued to rebel, supplying the unfortunate guests with a horrible smell. It overpowered the fresh smells of the bakery, but all I could do was stand there rigid and fight through it.

Customers came through the door, but I told them to wait. I couldn't help it anymore. I fled into the kitchen, once again feeling complete relief as soon as I crossed the threshold.

"Darian!" I growled. "He did this to me. When I get my hands on him..." I wrung them together, like I wanted to do right now.

Sally walked through the door, the smell of her cigarette clinging to her like a blanket.

"Who's watching the bakery?" she asked, casting me a glance.

"Take care of it," I snapped. "I can't go back in there." She went up to the window and looked through, then gave me a look. "That's not it."

"What is it--" she stopped, sniffing, then wrinkled her nose and turned.

"I can't help it," I wailed. "It's a long story."

She mumbled under her breath in another language, then walked out on me.

I busied myself with the scones, but couldn't bring myself to take them out, so I started on a batch of muffins. It was probably too late to sell them now, but there wasn't anything else I could do right now.

Not while he was out there.

I finished the muffins and started a loaf of bread by hand, mixing the ingredients and stewing over the predicament I put myself in. Twice. Or twice as bad.

The dough formed up, pale and white. I punched it down, kneading it with satisfaction. Over and over I smashed it, taking out my anger and frustration.

I was supposed to be lying low. Curse my own skill. I punched again, then sped up, starting to breathe hard.

"Sarah."

"What?" I spun, a lock of hair falling in my face.

"He's gone." I felt as deflated as the dough. It was ruined now, but I formed it into a loaf, anyway.

"Good riddance."

"You can't keep ignoring him forever."

"Why not?" Into the oven I tossed it with a clatter, the heat flushing into my face.

"It's a small town."

"Bah."

"You haven't gone anywhere since then, have you?"

I bristled. "Sure, I have."

"Besides your house." I didn't say anything, just stared. Thankfully, the bell rang.

"You have a customer."

Her lips pursed, her eyes shrunk. "Coming," she said in her most pleasant customer voice. "We'll continue this later," she whispered to me ominously.

I didn't want to talk about it, now or ever. Stomping over to the spice cabinet I retreated to my friends. Cinnamon, clove, allspice. These never let me down, never asked me to give up everything I loved in life to go work for him.

One by one I took them out and dusted them, carefully arranging them by height in groups. I loved the colors of all the caps, how it made an exciting tapestry.

I sighed and put them back, laying each one to rest like a baby. They were babies, my babies.

I wandered around the kitchen, at a loss. Should I go back and confront him? What would I say?

This place was my home now, had been for years. I didn't want to move again, uproot myself and go somewhere new and unknown.

What if they didn't like me? What if they found out? I chewed the side of my cheek, but decided there was nothing to do about it now.

I joined Sally in the front of the bakery, tending to the long line of customers that trickled to a stop just before closing.

Sally, gratefully, let me be. She was either too busy or sensed my discomfort. I might lose her too. The thought struck me like a weight.

Finally, I switched the sign at the door, looking out the window at the busy main street. Cars drove by, and a few people walked on the sidewalk under the hanging baskets of flowers the city had hung up on the light poles.

Were I to go back, this would all be a memory. A wonderful memory, but gone. I hugged myself.

"Now you talk," Sally said. I turned. She had assumed her most powerful stance, arms crossed, legs wide, and a scowl that could melt ice cream.

"I don't want to work for him."

"Then tell him that."

"You know I can't do that. He would end this place in a minute." I waved my hands around in a wide circle. All the work I had put into this place, the goods in the display cases, the mural of the meadow I had painted with my own hand. All of it would be gone.

"He is not so powerful."

"Sally, he was behind the closing of the Cowpoke Saloon. You know he hated the competition."

She scoffed. "That's a pack of rumors and whispers. No man has that power."

I shook my head. "This is no rumor." I couldn't tell her why I knew, without giving away my secret. "If I tell him no, then everything comes crashing down, we lose the bakery, and my life here is over." Exhausted, I slipped into a chair and hung a hand over my head.

"You're being dramatic again."

I peeked out from under my arm. "But what if it's worse? What if he..." I shuddered, "likes me?"

Sally's face contorted, then broke into peals of gruff laughter that sounded alien. It was like a full loaf of bread stuffed into a muffin. I made a face at her, but she was doubled over.

Finally, she stopped laughing. "I needed that," she said, wiping away small tears from the edge of her eyes.

"It's possible, you know."

"And I could be the Queen of England. You run a bakery, dear, not a restaurant. No restaurateur would call you competition."

But I knew better. There was a reason people flocked to the Buttered Loaf, and it wasn't for the large space and friendly atmosphere. Nor was it my baking skill alone.

"I've been up early," I said, ending the conversation and standing. "I'm going home, will you lock up please?"

"Did you clean up?" she asked as I pushed open the kitchen door. Dishes clogged the sink. I froze. There was more than a tone of warning in her voice.

"Er..." I trailed off, then sighed. There was no way out of this one. "I'll do them now."

My home was warm and inviting when I got back, fresh cinnamon filling the air. I pulled out a tub of ice cream as soon as I dumped everything. Triple Chocolate Chunk.

I considered baking a set of brownies, dreaming about how the fresh, piping hot chocolate dreams would melt the ice cream, dripping off in pools of pure delight.

But I settled for a spoon. The cold felt good on my tongue, and the chocolate was an explosion of taste to die for.

For not the first time I thought about getting a cat to welcome me home but dismissed it. It would remind me too much of the place I had left.

No, now I had a long night of worry and despair ahead of me and no place to go. I sunk into the couch and gazed down at my belly.

A little larger than it had been a few years ago. I poked it with the handle of my spoon. A little too jiggly.

I screwed up my face. *I'm not fat,* I told myself. But a piece of me lodged in the back of my brain, and I silenced it with another spoonful of ice cream.

I considered my options again. I could run, but that wouldn't be much better than my current situation. I had already tried to get help, and a fat lot of good that had done.

You could tell him the truth, a little voice on my shoulder whispered in my ear. *You might be surprised.*

And I might be the Queen of England myself. No, that was out.

I could stage my own death. Make it real tragic, enough to make all the old ladies bawl and moan. That would show them.

But then again, where would I go?

What if you struck back? Made the most powerful man in town work for you? I mused on the thought for a while, but the ice cream was melting around the edges and condensation trickled down my fingers.

I put it away and looked at the time. 3:45 pm. Still had hours until I could go to bed, despite the early baking hours I woke up at.

The Hallmark channel it was.

I flipped on the TV, but the voices just seemed to grate in my ear. It was another dumb plot line anyway, at least from what I could gather halfway in. Real women didn't even look like that.

I turned it off and paced around my couch. This shouldn't be that hard. Maybe Sally was right, maybe I should just tell him no. I blushed.

How was I supposed to do that now, with me and my...problem only when he was around?

Maybe that wasn't it, maybe it was pure coincidence and I was trying to convince myself to give me a nice excuse to avoid him.

I had to find out. I grabbed my keys and purse and went out. He should be at the Golden Homestead now, anyway. Plus, it was dinnertime, and I was craving a pork chop.

My heart was beating by the time I pulled up and parked. There it was the big neon dancing pig. My god, it was hideous. How did this man stay in business?

There was his Mercedes. I turned off the car, looking into my mirror to steady myself. "Just go in, see if it happens again, and come right back out. You only have to be there for a few minutes."

If it didn't happen, I'd stay for dinner. That wouldn't send any bad signals, right?

A pang of anger ran through me. Sally would laugh at me being attractive. To show her I put on my brightest red lipstick, putting on a nice pout for myself.

I was good looking, I was attractive. I slipped the lipstick away and calmed my breathing.

The smell of melting asphalt from the pavement rolled up when I opened my car, but I still went in through the two swinging doors.

"Howdy y'all, welcome to the Homestead. Glad you could make it back in for some down south cooking that'll make your mouth water." The bright-eyed blond dripped with a fake southern accent and seemed to bounce all over the hostess table. "Just one?" She paused with one menu and a beaming smile.

I looked around. He wasn't here. "Yes," I whispered. How was this going to work if he wasn't here?

I followed her in her too tight spandex pants to a booth. "Right in here y'all." I wanted to say something to wipe the smile off her face, but didn't.

"Thanks." My heart was beating a mile a minute. When she was gone I stood up slightly, peering over the edge of the booth. The bar had a few patrons, but no Peter. He must be in the kitchen.

"Howdy y'all," a voice said behind me. I jumped, banging my knees against the table, falling back into the booth, and smashing my head along the way. "That looked like it hurt, are you okay?" A server peered at me with a worried look on her face from under her cowboy hat.

"I'm fine." I held the back of my head with one hand and massaged my knees with the other. The server looked at me, then set down a glass of water and a plate of bread and butter.

"If you say so. I'm Nancy and I'll be your server this afternoon." Thankfully, no fake southern accent. "Can I start you off with our Blossoming Butter Bread or Terrific Taters and Cheese?"

"No thanks, I'm still thinking about it." I opened my menu and tried to get her to go away.

"Well, I'll give you a minute and let you peruse our victuals." I cringed, but she seemed totally unaffected. Like she had done this a thousand times before, which she probably had.

I nodded and she left me to nurse my wounds. I took a deep drink of the ice water, letting the cool flow into my mouth and down my throat. It felt good.

The restaurant had that stale oil smell so familiar with the deep-fried menu it came with. My arms stuck a little to the table, but when I pulled them away, it seemed clean under scrutiny.

Suddenly, my stomach growled and churned. I didn't feel so good.

"What are you doing here?" I started, let out a small yelp. Peter had snuck up behind me.

I squeezed my eyes shut as it began, realizing what a fool I had been.

"Having dinner. Is that okay?" I forced a smile, fighting desperately to keep it all inside, and failing. There was a small squeak.

Did he hear? I didn't think so. "I won't turn away a paying customer, but with the treatment you've been giving me I never expected to see you in here."

"Well, I get hungry sometimes," I said defensively.

He cocked his head to the side and raised one eyebrow. "Or are you here to finally give me an answer?" He crossed his arms and lifted his chin.

Sweat ran down my brows in trickles, small gasps of air escaped me. It took all my concentration to try to keep up with his words, if a bit late. "I, I--"

There it was, another one, and another building even bigger. It churned my insides to a pulp. I thought if I lifted my shirt, I would be able to see my stomach roiling like the rapids in the river. "I have to go."

I grabbed my purse, pushed him aside, despite his complaints, and rushed out the door, passing wind all the way.

Tears came to my eyes, of pure embarrassment. I pushed through the doors in a haze, not bothering to stop, and ran for my car.

My shoes flopped on the hot pavement, slapping me as the feeling inside fled. I was at the door and wrenched it open.

He had followed me to the door, stood saying something at me. I turned on the car and left as fast as I could.

So much for this experiment, failed and succeeded all in one. Only a few blocks away from my house did I regain my composure.

I let the car idle in the driveway, and then I banged on the steering wheel. "Stupid, stupid, stupid." I banged with every word, punctuating it.

Was my life falling apart before my very eyes? Or was I making too much out of it? I'm sure somewhere, someone had been through the same thing.

I desperately wanted somewhere to turn, someone to talk to. Someone who would understand me. But I was alone in this town. Even Sally could never know, as much as she knew about me, and my "gifts".

I sat there in the driveway for a long time. Thinking, and wondering, until the sun set and the streetlights flickered on, casting a hazy yellow glow across the run-down house.

I had to do it.

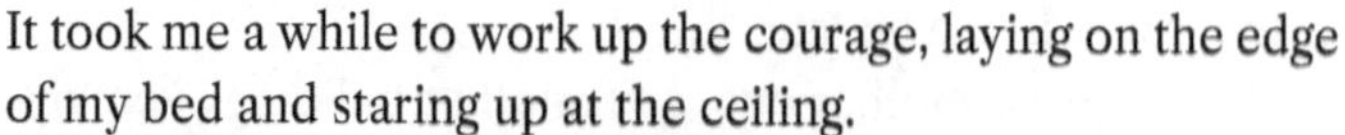

It took me a while to work up the courage, laying on the edge of my bed and staring up at the ceiling.

But when it was there, I took advantage of it and flew from my body to the cosmos. Through the planets and the stars, back to earth, until I ran through the forests and the meadows of my youth.

Until I came to the house at the edge of the woods.

Her house.

Smoke trailed out of its crooked chimney, blazing light from the windows in the dark of the night.

It was similar to what I remembered, and I floated, clutching my arms together even though the chill of the night could not reach me.

The door creaked open, and she stepped out. "Might as well come in."

Without a word I passed by her, two cups laid on the kitchen table by the hearty little fireplace with a kettle just beginning to whistle over it.

"You knew." She gave me a look, then pointed to the chair. "Have a seat."

"I don't know what to say." She took the kettle from the fire and poured it into the floral teapot. Roses, just like I remembered. I could almost smell the tea brewing inside as it sent up happy little puffs of steam. The lid went back on with a little click.

"Have you made your life, as you claimed?" My eyes shot to hers, there was victory in them, and pride. That riled my stubbornness.

"Yes. I've found my place, where people love me for who I am and what I do."

"Do they?" she leaned in closer. "Do they know who you really are?"

"The tea's ready," I said. Her eyes narrowed, then she pulled back her repressive body and took out the tea bags.

She poured two cups, all the good it would do, and I tried to grab mine.

My fingers went through, so I settled for pretending as she sipped hers with a contented sigh.

My mouth watered, tasting the floral concoction in my memory. I had never managed to perfect that recipe, no matter how hard I tried.

"I'm in a bit of trouble."

She snorted. "Tell me something I don't know."

"Have you been spying on me?"

She crooked a finger. "No need to spy when you broadcast yourself so loudly to the world a toddler on a trike couldn't miss."

Anger bubbled up inside. "I knew it, you wouldn't let me do this on my own. You put him up to this, didn't you?"

She shrugged. "Can't say one way or the other. I don't know what you mean."

"They'll find out this way. That's what you wanted, isn't it?" I felt my blood boiling, even though my body was miles away. My breathing was faster now.

"So, you hide it, do you?"

She had me caught. I cursed her wiles. "That's not the point. I've made a place for myself where I'm happy."

"Are you then? Is that why you sneak off in the night to Darian or fly here to me?" She set the teacup down with a clink. "It doesn't seem like you have it under control, let alone are happy."

I frowned. "What do you know about my life?"

"I know your predicament. That you decided to trust that old fool and let him help you." She made a spitting motion. "A fie upon him. And you, you'll learn your lesson well and you'll like it."

The flush burned my cheeks and threatened to rise to the top of my head, if I had one. "You aren't going to help me?"

"I'll help you the best way I know how." She squinted one eye and looked me up and down. "You've put on weight."

That was too much. I wanted to fly away, run back to my body and retreat into my home. Leave everything behind to sleep and ice cream and late-night Hallmark movies.

"Fine then." I hover stood up. "You stay here and be a crotchety old woman that no one loves."

Her eyes narrowed in anger. "You waste your skills, all that time you putter around the kitchen. All for what?" The tea stopped steaming. "To make others happy?" She bit off the last word with a wicked smile. "Go off, run like you always do. Maybe one day you'll grow a spine."

I turned and flew, not bothering to open the door. When I was back in my body, I curled up in the deepening afternoon light playing shadows on the wall. The wind whistled through the eaves, mocking me.

Nowhere left to go then, nowhere left to turn. *A spine.* The words throbbed in my ear, replaying over and over again.

And she was right.

All it would take were a few words, and it would fix everything. Or the right magic, in the right place at the right time.

But I couldn't even do that.

I wondered, thinking that I might be doing this on purpose. That my life was all about making my own life miserable.

That I was trying to become some sort of martyr to show her.

I wouldn't be some great sorcerer that Kings and Queens secretly sought after. No conjurer that fought armies and cast out demons.

No, I would just be a washed-up old woman living in a hut that no one loved. Maybe my cats would eat me.

I couldn't stand it anymore, and paced into the kitchen, some of the hurt turning to anger now.

That was what she wanted, and I was playing right into her hands.

The truth is, it wouldn't be bad working for Peter, but I would never be able to use my magic like I could with the bakery.

He had strong shoulders, as frustrating as he was to deal with. And the constant visits every day showed how tenacious he was, why he had succeeded so well in business.

I sighed, popped a frozen meal in the microwave, and slumped onto the island while it heated up.

I couldn't leave it. I couldn't let Sally down, or all my customers. They were happy, after they visited the bakery, and I knew it. She knew it, despite the hurtful words.

There was as strange touch of...pride in those words.

The microwave beeped, the overcooked smell of green beans and dehydrated potatoes wafted in the air. It was tasteless, so I added salt.

I finished my meal and went to bed, set the alarm clock for three, and laid eyes open.

Grow a spine. That was all I had to do.

It troubled me long into the night, but somehow, I fell asleep.

The alarm clock woke me with a jarring buzz in my ear. I slammed the snooze button, still clutching at the enticement of sleep and the fading memories of the dream.

A giant muffin, where had I got that into my head? And why was Peter there, half naked and shiny?

A gentle smile was on my lips, and as soon as I realized what I was thinking I wiped it off.

I could still feel the touch of his hands on my shoulders. Hard, firm hands from a lifetime of work and hard use.

I shuddered, some in pleasure and most in disgust, and hit my forehead. What was I thinking?

It was the day I would tell him no. That I never wanted to see his stinking face in my bakery again.

I sat up straight, shoulders back, and hands clenched in fists.

I'll show her.

With a big yawn I got out of bed and got ready for work. The night sky twinkled with a few stars that shone through the light pollution from the city.

This was my favorite time of day. No one was awake since it was too late for the night owls and too early for everyone else.

The roads were empty, and I sped to the bakery. I opened it up and turned on the lights, grateful for the silence of the morning.

With the ovens started and the smell of flour heavy in the air, I got to work.

Around me the machinery hummed, and I joined in. The mixer sang me a tune as it beat the dough for the breads, and I formed up the day's cookies by hand.

Each was imbued with everything I could make it, and no one was allowed in the kitchen while I was working.

The early risers would be in at six when the bakery opened, and the clock pointed to four when I pulled out the first of the breads and muffins.

When Sally walked in everything was ready and I was dusting my hands, a smile on my face.

"Good morning. How was your night?" I sang cheerfully.

"What's gotten into you?" She eyed me.

"Nothing, why do you ask?"

"You just seem a little..."

"Perky?" I suggested.

"Disingenuous." Her eyebrows were raised, and she crossed her arms.

"I don't know what you mean. Oh, look at the time. I'll get the sign." I took a pan of cookies with me and put it into the display case.

The regulars started trickling in, the early morning risers that gathered and talked over a few cups of coffee and bagels.

They were a loud group, but friendly enough, and were all retired and had nowhere else to go for the day.

"I'll help out this morning," I proclaimed, as the early rush trickled down.

"You aren't leaving?" Sally asked. It was unusual, but I had a spine now.

"It's a busy morning." There were no empty tables, but all the customers had been served.

"Right. What are you going to do when Peter comes in?"

"Oh, that." I trailed my finger along the clean counter. "I've made up my mind. I'm going to tell him to shove off. He can stick his job offer where the sun doesn't shine."

"Really?" The look she gave me wasn't encouraging.

"Yes. That's so."

She gave me a smile, cool despite the warmth of the bakery. "Then you shouldn't have any problem telling him now."

I glanced to where her eyes lead me, my stomach growling in warning. Peter pushed open the door, ringing the bell to announce his arrival.

And it started.

"Good morning," I said through clenched teeth, determined not to fail. This would be the one chance I had, I'm sure if I waited any more time my resolve would fail.

He greeted me with a suspicious look.

"Before I take your order," I said, as a squeaker escaped. "There's something I wanted to talk to you about."

"Go ahead." His eyes bored into mine. "I'm listening." His brown shirt complemented his eyes, sending a momentary flash of panic through me.

I swallowed, just as a loud one escaped. Blushing, I kept going, "Excuse me. It's about your offer." This fart was louder, and he definitely noticed. Now, a flush crept up on his cheeks.

Something changed. Now, he was embarrassed, too. We were suddenly on equal footing, and I let go.

"Excuse me again." They kept coming, and now the whole bakery was looking at me, Sally a hand over her face. "I'll have you know I love what I do, and I can't do it for you." A loud one rippled through the building. "Pardon."

I'll show her. The one sliver of stubbornness in my body kept me going. "I won't work for you, Mr. Framton, and I decline your offer of employment." A satisfying fart punctuated the end.

"Well," he said, rubbing his head in some form of self-soothing. "I can respect that."

"Excuse me," I said as I farted again.

"If you change your mind, and I hope you do, please let me know." He ordered through my flatulence, but I held my head high. In short order, he had been outfitted with a raspberry scone and two bagels, paid, and sent on his way.

I wanted to crawl into a hole, but at the same time I was triumphant. A little embarrassment wasn't going to stop the life I had built here.

He was almost gone, hand at the door, and I was ready for it, when he paused and turned back to me.

His normally confident eyes looked different, almost afraid. "I have a confession. I only wanted to get you to work for me because I like," the word caught in his throat, "and admire you. Would you consider coming to dinner with me sometime?"

My mouth dropped, and it took me a moment to pick it up off the floor.

What kind of reversed world was I living in? Had the sky turned to the sea and lions walked with lambs?

"Yes." The word escaped my lips almost as easily as the farts escaped my body, and then he smiled and was gone.

My heart a flutter, the discomfort went and the memory was just a fart on the breeze, but left its lingering stench.

"You did it. I'm impressed." Sally was giving me an appraising eye. "Although I could do without the fireworks."

"I can't help it. It only happens around him."

"That will be an interesting date, then." She shut the register with a click, and it hit me.

What had I gotten myself into?

3

VISIONS AND THE GREAT TREE

"Step forward." Turning to the rest of the men the elder asked the assembled "Is there one who will act as this young one's guide?" Braun, Danny's father, stepped forward.

"Aye, I will guide him." He boomed. One of the tallest men in the village, he towered above the elder. The elder nodded and turned back toward Treflin. Braun stepped out of the line and took his place behind Treflin, squeezing his shoulder with his massive hands reassuringly. Without a word, the elder turned, and the men circled around Treflin and began to walk forward. Treflin began to follow the elder, who stepped off and led the circle forward. Silently they all began to tread their way to the north end of the square, following the road that led out of town. They made their way past the makeshift market stall area of town, where the villagers set up wares on the weekend to barter and trade for others crafted item. Just after they had exited the village the group stopped, and the elder turned toward him and nodded to one of the men. Treflin felt him slip a rough sack over his head, completely restricting his view. Surprised, Treflin immediately felt a panic roll through his body, but quickly forced it down with the help of a reassuring hand from Braun gently placed on his shoulder. Treflin was now entirely dependent on him, not being able to see anything, and felt helpless. With a gentle push from Braun, he began to walk forward again, hesitantly following. The path was smooth but even so Treflin would find his feet caught on something, nearly falling.

Following the road out of town the walked for what seemed to Treflin to be an eternity. Fully disoriented, it felt like they were leading him through the mountains. At several points Braun stopped him to step over large logs. His footsteps through the fallen leaves and undergrowth told him they had left the path for the forest at some point, and he smelled the deep, earthy woods that told him they were off the beaten path. It felt as though they were going round in circles, even though he had a relatively good sense of direction. *What will happen to me?* he wondered to himself. *And where are they taking me?* Treflin was familiar with the woods around the village, as a favorite playtime spot as a child. Soon enough, they stopped his bumbling wandering.

"Remove your clothing," Treflin heard the elder say. They did not remove the hood, its rough, scratchy wool still blocking all view. Treflin hesitated, and then began unlacing his shirt. Braun assisted him in removing it from his torso, careful to not remove the hood and keep him blind. Awkwardly, now half naked, Treflin fumbled at his laces on his boots, removing them, followed by his trousers. Treflin finally removed his socks and stood there, waiting.

"All clothing." The elder said. Forced by the weight of his words, Treflin fully disrobed through his extreme embarrassment. Excepting the woolen hood, he was completely naked, standing in the forest. He felt a tugging at the hood, and it was removed.

Blinking at the suddenly blinding light, Treflin realized he was standing in the middle of a small, circular clearing in the forest. In the center stood a massive old tree stood, one Treflin did not recognize. Treflin gaped at its largeness, how it reached up to the sky and reached out over the canopies of the smaller trees. Lowering his eyes back to the elder he realized the clearing was surrounded by the men of the village, and again remembered his nakedness, attempting to cover himself with his hands. The elder held a glowing candle in the soft darkness beneath the tree.

"A man enters the world naked." The elder intoned, clearly a practiced ceremony he had performed many times before.

"A man enters the world alone." The men around the ring responded in unison, their voices chilling Treflin to the bone. Braun stepped from behind him, holding a dark brown cloak in his arms.

"Be clothed." Braun said to him, offering the cloak to him. Treflin took it from his hands and quickly pulled it over his head, wanting to be covered as quickly as possible. Braun stepped back and gestured for Treflin to move forward to a small stone circle embedded in the clearing. Treflin nervously stepped up and took his place in the center of the clearing. The elder continued to stand with his candle, the flame dancing on the end of the wick. One by one the men of the village continued the ritual, stepping forward and speaking.

"Belinda, Geoffry, Sam, Sarah." The blacksmith intoned and then stepped back into the circle. Farmer Macel, the next in line, stepped forward.

"Prance, Cherish." Farmer Macel, the next man in line said, returning to his place. On and on the men went, around the circle speaking names. Treflin realized a few men in that they were naming all the members of their household, wondering what it all meant. The men reverently said their names aloud each time, the words drifting on the soft breeze traveling through the forest. There was a rhythm humming through their words, weaving and tying it all together in Treflin's mind. He felt entrapped by it, mesmerized by the words as he stared at the candle. Braun, the last man, stepped forward and finished the ritual.

"Priscilla, Saul, Danny, Paul, Heather, Francis, Talia, Dreft, Sprance, Treflin." At his name Treflin started, caught off guard. He was not in Braun's family. It made him think, perhaps it was part of the ritual? All men complete, the elder stepped forward, now less than a foot from him.

"Do you wish to be a man?" The elder asked. Treflin felt the anxiety and weight behind what his next words would be. Mouth dry, he licked his lips and responded.

"Yes."

"Then you will be tested." The elder replied, the force of his words descending on Treflin and striking fear into his heart. Even though he was at least a foot taller than the elder, he was still looking up at him beneath that gaze. The men began to depart, filing into a single line. Treflin realized why he had never seen this portion of the forest as they left, it was completely surrounded by an impenetrable layer of brambles seven feet high. Treflin tried to watch the men but the elder blowing out the candle caught his attention and brought him back into focus. Soon they were left, just the elder, Braun, and himself. Braun, pointing up to the top of the tree brought his attention to it.

"Do you see that mushroom growing up there?" Braun asked. Noticing it halfway up the tree trunk, Treflin nodded. Treflin also noticed odd protrusions that randomly made their way up the relatively straight, massive trunk. "You need to climb the Great Tree and collect a mushroom. Once you have it, you need to descend safely back to the ground with the mushroom and return it to the elder."

The elder walked over to a small stump and plopped himself down. Treflin looked back up at the tree. He was used to climbing trees, especially when he was younger, but he did not have a lot of practice lately, with needing to watch after the farm. Braun also took a seat on a log that looked like it was placed there to be a seat. Treflin walked over to the base of the tree. At first, he did not think that the mushroom was that far up the tree, but after he got closer, he realized just how far up it was. Standing at the base he peered up the trunk, searching out a path up to the monstrously tall trunk.

It seemed to be darker at this point of the clearing, although there was plenty of light to see everything. He felt small, and afraid in its shadow, and stood at the bottom attempting to muster his courage. Reaching out one hand he touched the bark of the tree and recoiled in horror. The tree itself was warm! Treflin turned back to the elder and Braun, who waved him onward, and turned back to the tree itself.

Reaching out his hand once more he touched the tree. It was rough like a normal tree trunk, but it was warm to the touch, an odd sensation that sent a chill down his spine. Feeling the same cowardice he felt last night he stubbornly mustered up all the courage he had. Grinding his teeth in determination he told himself *I will not be a coward like I was last night.* He reached out his other hand and grabbed one of the protrusions. It too felt warm, and also rough, but not like the bark was. It felt as though the tree itself had grown a place for his hand to rest. Cautiously he found another handhold and grabbed on, then testing the weight of the hold, he put his foot on a lower protrusion. Not having put his boots back on he again felt the odd squirming sensation in his stomach as his bare foot touched the warm bark, but it gave his foot plenty of purchase. Now, fully involved, he reached his other foot up to a higher protrusion and looked up, beginning to climb.

Even though the height was much more than he originally anticipated he made quick progress in the beginning. Steadily he put one foot up, shifted his weight, and moved his opposite hand up, searching for the next handhold. He quickly grew accustomed to the warm bark, even pleasantly surprised at the warmth radiating from it to his body. The rough woolen cloak trapped in his body heat and quickly made him sweat. The sweat collected on his body, particularly on his back, and the scratchy wool began to make him itch. Not having a hand free to do anything about it Treflin simply ignored the sensation and kept concentrating on the task at hand. Slowly, but surely, he made his way up the tree, inching his way closer to the goal. He was about ten feet away from the mushroom when he made his first mistake, stopping to gauge the distance he had covered. Looking down toward the ground made him realize just how far up he had come, and how far down the fall was if he was to let go. As if on cue, his mind began its nervous race. A feeling of vertigo rushed through his body, and he became uncomfortably aware of how exposed he was. Immediately his body reacted by crouching closer to the tree, as if to gain comfort from its proximity, but it did nothing to calm his mind. Averting his gaze back to the tree Treflin focused on the rough bark, feeling his heart pounding in his chest and realizing how quickly he was breathing. An ache of exhaustion began to creep into his forearms, unused to holding on to such a precariously handhold. Treflin realized, through the adrenaline, that he needed to hurry. Focusing all his willpower into just moving he began to repeat a mantra in his head. *Keep going, you are almost there*, he said to himself, repeating it over and over again, focusing on the words and not how far up he was. If he were to let go, he would be crushed like a bug on the rocky ground just below him.

Soon he found that his handholds were no longer appearing within his reach. Realizing he had finally met his goal Treflin looked at the mushroom just inside his reach for the first time. It was unlike any other he had seen before, a cluster of half plate-like mushrooms that were dark brown on the top, spotted with black stains, which appeared to be giving off an extremely slight glow on the bottom. He reached out his hand and grabbed a medium-sized one growing near the bottom of the group, not surprised to find it was covered in a thin, sticky substance. Giving a tight tug, as he hung suspended in the air off the side of a tree trunk, he found that it came off the trunk relatively easily and basked in a quick moment of triumph. Then, he realized, he had not thought of how he was going to carry it down.

Panicking, he craned his head around his body, looking at the robe he was wearing. It had no pockets, or hood, or anything else that would have been remotely useful for carrying a mushroom while hanging off the side of a tree. It was just a simple piece of cloth. For a moment he considered dropping the mushroom down to the ground but realized that most likely would have resulted in a failure of the test. Breathing deeply, he considered his options. He was halfway up the side of a tree with no way of carrying a mushroom, carrying a mushroom, and his arms were becoming more tired by the moment. Taking one more deep breath, inspiration struck him. There was only one way to carry the mushroom down.

Treflin put the mushroom in his mouth and bit down gently to keep it there. It tasted terrible, like a mixture of rotten eggs and a month-old dead body rolled into one, and the slime immediately coated his mouth and began to force its way down his throat, almost making him gag. Eyes watering with the unpleasantness Treflin grabbed back onto his perch, feeling relief for his arm holding up his weight, and quickly began making his way down the trunk in reverse, feeling his way down with a foot for purchase, testing it, and then moving the opposite arm and repeating. It was slower to go down than it was going up as he could not see below him and the mushroom in his mouth prevented him from getting a good view down, so he made his way down by feel only. He had only descended a few feet down when odd things began to happen.

At first it started as a slight shrill wind, but then the noise developed into what he thought could only be described as a long, thin voice. It was as if someone was talking to him from a great distance, yelling, but you could not quite make out what they were saying. The shrill noise turned into a low moan, tickling his ears and putting him on edge. Treflin felt as though he could feel eyes drilling into his back, but couldn't turn to look because he was too involved in trying to climb down. His legs were burning now as well as his arms, his toes roughed by the bark of the tree. He wanted to look down to see how much farther he had to go but he knew that if he did, he might not be able to make it down. The odd noise on the wind grew more and more clear, although he could still not make out what it was saying. Sweat and wool prickling his body, he continued the long slog down, focusing on just moving one limb at a time. His arms were shaking now, exhausted from the effort of holding up his body, and muscles he did not even know existed were burning. The mushroom in his mouth was getting more difficult to hold on to, his saliva turning the already slippery mushroom even more slippery. He had to start stopping to adjust it, taking precious seconds from his trek.

Soon he felt as though he could just make out the words on the wind, so he concentrated intently on them. With a start, he realized it sounded like someone was calling his name.

"Treflin..." it said in a deep, low voice, unnerving him and sending chills down his spine. The wind blew through the trees, rustling the leaves vigorously, but did not appear to affect the tree he was climbing. The light coming in the clearing seemed to darken, taking on a deep red hue. Treflin sped up, trying to complete his task as he worked through the burning in his limbs, but misplaced his foot and had it slip off the protrusion. The sudden shift in his weight broke his grip on his right hand and he felt his other foot lose its purchase. Instinctively he held on for dear life with his left hand, thankfully keeping him from falling. Hanging precariously, he found himself looking down at the ground, hope fading in his heart as he realized how high up he still was.

Stomach lurching in his chest and fingers slipping off the protrusion, Treflin scrambled to grab back on with his other hand. He reached out and felt his hand make contact. Scrambling with his legs, he managed to latch back onto the tree, saving himself from falling the remaining distance to his death. Breathing heavily through his nose, he choked down another wave of bitter vile from the mushroom and pushed himself to keep going.

Keep going. Treflin repeated to himself over and over. The voice on the wind, ever so faint, continued to call to him, and the itching cloak dug deeper into his body. He was sweating a river now, soaking into the cloak and adding to the discomfort, but he kept going. Looking up the tree at where he had come from, he noticed something odd in the dark at the top of the canopy. Legs and arms burning and shaking he continued down, shooting one more glance at the movement that caught his eye. There was something in the shadows, moving, but he could not make it out quite all the way, it had gotten so dark.

He peered up, stopping to catch his breath even though he knew it would be taxing on his already exhausted body, the cloak soaking up his sweat and weighing him down. He peered up into the tree and thought he saw the moving object once more, only this time he could make it out. Treflin blinked his eyes, making sure they were seeing what he was seeing. Not understanding what he was looking at, he eyed what looked like a snake coming down the tree trunk from the shadows. Treflin, fear growing in his heart, continued to descend the tree, glancing up into the canopy every once in a while. The object made its way down the tree too until it had finally entered a shaft of light breaking through the cover and illuminating the tree trunk. Treflin recoiled in horror, nearly losing his grip again, to see that it was not a snake, but a thick vine snaking its way down the tree, moving by itself. He knew that the vine was coming for him, covering in sinister leaves and long thorns dripping some wet substance. The fear motivated Treflin to continue, and he was able to force his head into an uncomfortable position that gave him the ability to see where he was going to put his feet, and also afforded him a view that was still very far down, if it was less than before.

Panicked and exhausted Treflin continued the trial down the Great Tree, alternating between glancing up at the vine and seeing his way down. He realized that not only was the vine going faster than he was, but that more vines had joined the first, thicker and knottier than the first he had seen. Pure panic and fear filled his mind as the vines approached him, at first twenty feet away, and then 10, the painfully slow climbing hampering his ability and putting more fear in his mind. Treflin realized as the vines began to close faster and the ground not getting any closer that he was not going to beat it to the bottom, and beyond exhaustion, finally made his last mistake, his hand slipping away causing him to lose all grip and tumble away from the trunk. As he fell Treflin closed his eyes and accepted his fate.

The vines shot forward, wrapping themselves around his body, their thorns piercing his skin and sending searing pain at the punctures. They clung to his arms and legs. Treflin felt them close about his body, quickly halting his downward descent with a jar. Pain running through his body Treflin realized he was still alive, having fallen the last portion of the tree and rescued at the last second. The vines stretched one last time, placing his tired body on the ground, and seemed to shrivel up, releasing him from their grasp and depositing him onto the rocky grass. Treflin watched in wonder as they receded back up into the canopy of the Great Tree, and touched his face with trembling fingers to see if he still was alive. The fog in his mind lifted as he realized what he was supposed to do, and momentarily forgetting the incredible supernatural event he had managed to live through, panicked to find the mushroom that was the mission of his folly. It was still there in his mouth, and he took it out, fascinated to see only teeth marks had made an impression on the skin of the mushroom, his deep bite not able to break through its skin.

He lay there for a moment longer, catching his breath and relishing the feeling of being alive, just feeling the blood coursing through his body. He had somehow lived through the horrible event, unbeknownst to him how. An act of providence had reached down to save him. Hands still shaking from exertion, he attempted to rise to his feet, rolling over onto his side and cradling the mushroom like a baby. He managed to get into a kneeling position, but found his legs were too exhausted to be able to bring him to his feet so he sat there for a few seconds. A hand, Braun's hand, reached out to him and hoisted him to his feet by grabbing him under the arm. Once he stood precariously, and Braun supported him by taking his free hand and wrapping it around his shoulder, Treflin found that he could hobble. Grateful to Braun, but both silent, Treflin and Braun made their way back to the elder who was still sitting in the spot Treflin had left him in, only now he had a small pestle and mortar in his lap. They stopped in front of the elder and Braun gestured for him to offer the mushroom. Treflin obliged, handing over the precious thing to the elders outstretched arm, dropping in the mortar he held for him. Quickly the elder began crushing the mushroom, the odor released and wafting up for Treflin to smell. It smelled of fresh rain in the morning, and damp earth, but there were also subtle hints of bad smells hidden throughout. The colorful mushroom quickly turned into a dull gray paste in the mortar under the elder's practiced hands. Once complete he pulled out a small glass vial from a pocket in his garb and opened the stopper and poured it in the mortar, mixing it all together. The entire thing had turned into a dull gray liquid, somewhat thick and not runny. The elder poured the concoction into a crude wooden cup engraved with strange markings Treflin had never seen before, perhaps an old language.

"From one generation to the next, we pass." The elder intoned, and then offered the cup to Treflin. Recovered enough to stand on his own, Treflin felt Braun remove his support for him to step forward. Treflin took the offered cup and looked at it, not wanting to do what he thought the elder was going to ask him to do. "For the protection of the village you come of age." The elder said and nodded to the cup.

Treflin took a deep breath, mustering his courage and resolve, and raised the cup to his lips. He drank of it, tasting the vile fluid as it hit his mouth and almost spitting it back out. Tears in the corners of his eyes from the bad taste he continued to drink it, feeling it clump together in his throat and making its way down into his belly. It was the most disgusting thing he had tasted, even more so than the taste of the raw mushroom on his descent. Choking it down he finished the cup, coughing from the taste. Almost immediately he felt a huge rush of vertigo and his world open up, time slowing down. The elder stood, as if in slow motion, and walked away, Braun following him, leaving Treflin alone in the clearing. Treflin staggered a few steps and then collapsed to his knees, feeling odd sensations rolling through his body. Unable to support himself anymore Treflin slumped to the ground and drifted off into a drug induced slumber.

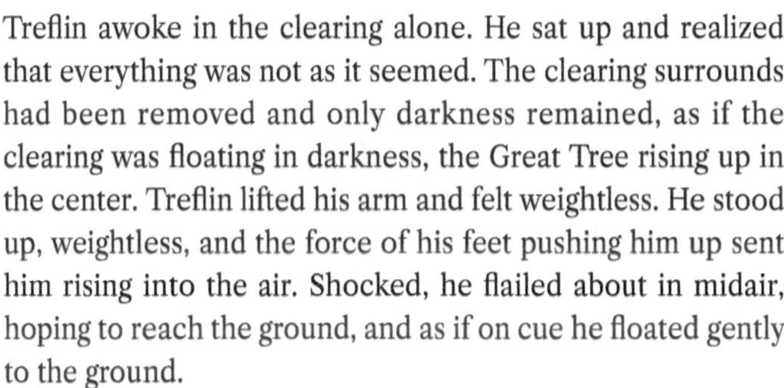

Treflin awoke in the clearing alone. He sat up and realized that everything was not as it seemed. The clearing surrounds had been removed and only darkness remained, as if the clearing was floating in darkness, the Great Tree rising up in the center. Treflin lifted his arm and felt weightless. He stood up, weightless, and the force of his feet pushing him up sent him rising into the air. Shocked, he flailed about in midair, hoping to reach the ground, and as if on cue he floated gently to the ground.

"Where am I?" Treflin asked out loud, his voice echoing throughout the darkness. "What am I doing here?" He expected no answer and got none. Wondering what he was supposed to do he began to pace back and forth, trying to figure out his conundrum. On a pivot around his foot that brought him to face away from the tree he jumped, startled at a figure that had suddenly appeared. It looked like a person in golden armor, with a long white cloak flowing behind it and just draping against the ground. The armor was beautiful and instantly mesmerized him, curved and gentle but clearly made to withstand damage. Perched at the top the helmet resembled that of a demonic head, antlers flowing from the top and a gruesome face twisted in pain or disgust.

"You are where you need to be." A voice emanated from the helmet. "As for your other question." The figure shrugged. "You will have to figure that one out for yourself." Treflin realized his jaw had dropped and his mouth was hanging open, so he quickly shut his mouth. He was too surprised to be frightened at first, but now he became wary, not sure of the man's intentions, at least he thought it was a man from the deepness of his voice.

"Who are you?" Treflin croaked out, his voice cracking with the stress. He had curled back as the figure talked, adopting a form of protection without realizing it.

The figure slowly raised his hand, brushing past an ornate hilt of what looked like a very large sword and fixed is hands firmly on the helmet. Giving a slight tug the man, and Treflin could see it was a man, pulled off of his helmet.

"I am a helper, a guide of sorts." The man replied, shifting the helmet to one hand and cradling it beneath his arm. "The name I was given is Harrison Fjord, but that is long beneath me." With a wave of his hand, the helmet disappeared and a table dissolved into existence in front of him.

He had hit a brick wall, unable to continue down the same path he was going to walk down. Treflin realized that he was in some sort of odd dream, but was not quite sure what made him feel that way or how he got there. The fear he felt originally of Harrison quickly faded, however, and he began to calm down. He walked closer, or at least tried to.

His light weighted-ness made him float on his toes, although willing himself to get heavier somehow tended to help. He approached the table and two chairs appeared, Harrison pulling one out.

"Care for a drink?" Harrison asked, a strange silver cylinder appearing in his hand, odd lettering on it with mountains magically painted in the background. The lifelike nature of the mountains made Treflin stare, wondering what artist could do something that lifelike. There were women in the village who liked to add paintings to clothes and containers, but nothing that good. Spellbound, it took Harrison repeating his question to bring him back to the conversation. Treflin felt like he was being thrust in every direction, overwhelmed at the strangeness of it all. Remembering the vile concoction he had swallowed, Treflin declined.

"Who are you?" Treflin asked, although a small part of him thought it was a silly question. Some inkling in his mind told him he already knew the answer to the question, which confused him even more. Harrison chuckled, noticing the look on Treflin's face.

"It can be confusing, I know," Harrison said. "But we are not here for questions like that, we do not have time for it." He suddenly seemed very serious, leaning forward across the table seemingly growing bigger. "This is a time for action."

Suddenly everything around them was gone, they were somehow transported to the edge of a cliff, overlooking a large valley. Treflin gasped at how high up they were, the valley floor covered in trees. The trees were moving individually, catching his eye. He looked closer and realized it was two armies arrayed on a battlefield before him. One of light, and one of dark.

"The world was once overcome by darkness." Harrison told him, gesturing to the dark army. It was vast, a giant sea of bodies rolling over the valley, fuming and frothing. "The hearts of men turned from good to the evil inside them." An evil mist rose up behind the dark army, creeping its way through the mass, pulsing with a dark light that sought to overcome. It seemed to strengthen the dark army, make it grow.

"There were few who rejected the evil, and fewer still to stand against it," Harrison said, gesturing to the small army standing in opposition. Compared to the other it was relatively small and weak, vastly outnumbered by the dark army. "They chose to stand against all odds." The two armies stopped, drawing up in battle lines. There was a pause as they faced off and Treflin could feel the overwhelming despair that the men must have felt staring down their death. He imagined the life ahead of him, the quiet farm, maybe marrying one of the village girls and settling down to have children of his own, and imagined that being ripped away from him by war. The thoughts of the night before came back to him; the plea of Melcadiah, the strength of Danny, the tender touch of Tilda.

Once more their surroundings shifted only to bring them into the thick of the light army. They were surrounded by men, too old and too young to fight, a ragtag band of misfits. They were precious few professional soldiers mixed into the group.

"Brace!" he heard a voice cry out, one of the leaders no doubt. Treflin looked to the front of the group as they assumed a fighting stance, oddly precise and well-practiced. The onslaught had begun. The dark wave of forms rushed forward, pulsing with the tendrils of haze dispersed throughout, feeding them.

"We made our stand here." Harrison said, attracting Treflin's attention. Looking at him Treflin could see he had changed, no longer wearing the shining armor he had appeared in, only clad in simple armor, much more than his compatriots. "Side by side we fought the tide of darkness, and were nearly overwhelmed." The first wave struck the front lines, tearing and cutting. Miraculously the line held, men falling and being replaced by more, stepping into the gaps, the fallen pulled back to the rear of the line. Harrison slowly lowered the visor of his helmet, shutting it with a clang that ran out in the melee. The clash of steel on steel and screams of men wounded and dying nearly overwhelmed Treflin, the smell of sweat and dust mixed with blood and the excrement of the dead as they evacuated themselves. Even though he could tell it was not real, like some sort of dream or vision, Treflin felt himself caught up in the excitement and fear of the situation, heart pumping for action. He felt a hand on his shoulder and turned to see an old man, eye covered in a bandage, offering him a spear. Treflin looked at him, and then at the spear, confused. If this was a dream, how was the man able to see him or hear him?

"All men die." Harrison continued, drawing his sword. It glimmered in the light shining from the sun behind them, lancing out rays of light to pierce through the fog before them that was drawing down on them. "You must choose how to live, to stand and fight, or to run away." The army had broken through the front ranks now, and was quickly approaching their position, striking down everyone before them in their path. A large form, nearly double the height of all the men, was hacking his way toward them, leading a group clad in black against the men of light. Treflin was frozen, the man still standing before him offering a weapon, the enemy approaching him. He knew he had to take up the spear, but he was afraid. Caught in between a rock and a hard place he felt his impending doom approach. The large fighter was clad in night black armor, pointy and spiked, standing twice as tall as any man. He carried a sword in one hand, like a large extended butcher's knife, and a dull, evil mace in the other, swinging them wide and often into the crowd. The army scrambled to get away, parting in front of them and leaving a clear path to Treflin. The world slowed, the moments turning into eternity. The enemy arrived in front of him, throwing everyone else aside and stopped. The enormous sword rose into the air, poised to make its final descent.

Without thinking Treflin took the spear. The sword descended. Treflin closed his eyes and threw up the spear in defense. Metal struck metal and a bright light burst forth from the spear. It blossomed in his eyes, making Treflin open them. Above him the sword had met the spear in midair, stopping it a mere hairs breadth from his face. A while light pulsed from it, sending its waves outward, melting the darkness. The enemy was thrown back by the light, and it pushed away the evil fog, cleansing it from the earth, taking the dark army with it. The white light became too bright to look at, and everyone shielded their eyes.

"Open your eyes lad." Harrison said. Treflin opened his eyes, seeing a battlefield emptied of the enemy. Aghast, Treflin realized that he had done it all, and felt bile rise into his throat. He tried to keep down the contents of his stomach, but failed, turned to wretch into the bloodstained grass. The army was gathering around him, a crowd looking at him. There were wounded and alive alike, being supported by each other where they needed to, and as Treflin rose back on his feet with the help of the spear, he noticed them all looking at him.

"Our hope has come." The old man who had given him the spear said, weeping on his knees. Treflin realized that they were talking about him and immediately became terrified. He took a step back, then another, backing up away from the crowd.

"No, no." Treflin replied. He realized he was holding the spear that had done it, still in his hands.

"The Hero!" Another man cried out. Whispers rippled through the crowd, more eyes fixated on him. Treflin looked around, his head whipping this way and that like a cornered dog.

"No!" Throwing down the spear, Treflin turned and ran. He did not want this, this vision. He had the village, his farm, his brother to look after, not these men. The battlefield rippled away and once more Treflin found himself in the clearing alone with Harrison.

"I stood that day where you were," Harrison told him, once more arrayed in his magnificent armor. The table was gone, and they stood facing each other, his cape rippling with an unseen breeze.

"I'm not that man, I can't be," Treflin replied, numb and shell-shocked. He felt himself being ripped from this world as his body fought the poison coursing through his body. There was little time and Harrison just smiled a knowing, sad smile as Treflin faded from view, waking from his drug induced slumber.

"No one ever is."

4

STEELEYES IN THE DARK

A happy tune whistled through the mountain path, followed by the dwarf whistling it. He had a pack on his back and a spring in his step.

And a short sword sheathed on his hip.

His steps took him up the craggy mountain path, worn by generations of goats.

At the peak he stopped and breathed deep, surveying the mountains below. The mountains rose up beside a river, deep sentries that sharpened to little points capped with white.

The evergreen forests crept up their sides, stopped at the timberline by a suffocating lack of oxygen and earth that transformed into dirt.

Barileth, the dwarf, set down his pack and gathered a few sticks into a fire. In no time he had it crackling and spitting, whipped by the wind.

A frying pan followed, and meat joined it. Into the fire they went, and soon it was sizzling. Barileth shuffled the meat around the pan, careful to keep it from burning.

Up ahead of him a figure appeared on the path, but Barileth paid it no heed. It grew closer, a man, clad in thick winter gear. Their eyes met for a moment, but Barileth returned to his work.

"Hullo," the stranger called as he approached the makeshift camp.

Barileth grunted and turned the meat over.

"May I share your fire?"

"Keep to yourself."

"Please," the man said, shivering in the wind that whipped up from the valley, bringing with it a chill and smell of the evergreens below, thick and heady. His teeth were chattering. "I'm so cold up here."

Barileth narrowed his eyes. Then, after a long, pregnant pause, he nodded.

The man sighed with relief and approached, reaching out with knobbly fingers. Smoke blew in his eyes, but he didn't seem to care. It gave Barileth cover to examine him more closely.

He was tall in comparison to Barileth, but short for a human man. A hat covered his hair, and a coat his figure, but his fingers were thin.

The meat was finished and giving off a wonderful aroma. Barileth stabbed a piece with his knife and lifted it to his lips, blowing off the steam that came from it.

The man's eyes followed it to his mouth, devouring it in looks. Barileth bit into it, warmth and juice flooding his lips, and chewed. The man licked his lips.

"I've shared my fire with you," Barileth said after swallowing his mouthful. "Don't expect anything else."

"I'm called Seth, from the farther reaches of Guzan to the south. Have you heard of it?" Seth seemed to have recovered some of his strength with the warmth.

Barileth grunted and took another piece of meat. The man stared at it longingly, but reached into his pack and pulled out a cloth-wrapped package. He opened it, revealing a half-eaten loaf of bread.

"I have bread to trade, if you'd accept it." Seth proffered the bread. Barileth stared at it as he chewed.

He reached into the pan and carved off a slice of the meat. Barileth popped it into his mouth and smiled.

Seth's face fell. He wrung his hands. "There's...something else I can offer."

Barileth perked up. His imagination started running.

A simple trade. *I have enough food. Why not give him what he wants?*

"I'll need your word, and something more than that, to be able to trust you."

"You have it."

"And the something else?"

The man tensed up, clearly salivating over the meat. Barileth jiggled the pan, showing how tasty it looked. He bit his lip, then looked to the ground.

"I—I know where a treasure lies."

"You have my attention." Barileth sat up, eyes flashing into action. Visions of gold, of jewels, of great stores of weapons flashed through his mind.

But then caution prevailed. *How easy it is for humans to lie, how hard it is for them to follow up on their word.* "What is treasure to you may not be treasure to me."

Barileth carved off another piece and ate it in front of him.

"It's an enchanted amulet," the man said, crawling forward. "It bestows upon its owner great luck."

"Luck, eh?"

"Yes." He nodded furiously. "And I can take you to where it lies, ripe for the plucking."

"You'll tell me where it is, then you get your food."

He didn't like it, and Barileth saw the anger flash across his face, but his hunger was too great. He nodded.

"A cave, along this way, to the south. I know where it is and how to get in." He looked like he wanted to continue. "My name is Seth Lothorin."

Satisfied, Barileth cut him a piece and tossed it to him. "Barileth Steeleyes."

Seth snatched it out of the air, devouring it like a starving wolf would a helpless deer. Juice ran down his lips, and with two fingers he wiped and licked it clean.

"And what else do you know about this...cave?"

"It's guarded by monsters. Fell beasts that walk in the night but are asleep during the day."

"You lied to me then." Barileth's eyes narrowed. He pulled back his food.

"No, I tell you the truth now." The food was working, bringing some life back to the poor beggar's cheeks. "The great Lady has shown favor upon me, bringing me to you, for not only have you provided me food longed for, you also can accompany me and help clear out the guardians of the treasure."

A cold wind whistled through the mountains, rattling the trees down lower in the valley. An eagle screamed overhead, drifting lazy circles in pursuit of its prey.

Barileth had taken a chance, and now found himself in an unenviable position. Men were not trustworthy, and this one seemed less so.

"Take me there." Barileth gave him the rest of the meat, taking bread out of his pack and dividing it up among them. "And tell me everything you know."

Soil crunched underfoot as they left the beaten path farther down the mountain. Seth Lothorin, for that was the man's name, pointed to the peak to the east. "It's at the foot of that mountain, hidden in a valley obscured from the path."

"All things are hidden up here. That's why I chose it." Barileth followed the man, keeping a close eye on him, but he seemed to be telling the truth, and the path they traveled checked out with everything else he had said.

He was starting to relax. Not much, but enough to take the man at his word.

The food had given him strength, enough to see that the sword slung at his hip was more than an accessory to keep the brigands at bay. He walked with a grace and pace that screamed fighter.

Still, the tales he had to tell seemed more than fantastic to Barileth.

"And why did you seek the hidden path, Master Steeleyes?" Seth glanced back to read his expression.

Barileth kept his face clean of emotion. "I haven't asked about your plans."

"Point taken. Here." He pointed off the path to a relatively flat spot. "We can camp here for the night and go the rest of the way in the morning." He squinted, judging the distance to the mountain. "It should only take half the morning, plenty of time to get in and out before they even know what's happened."

Barileth settled down, sloughing his pack off to one side. They were sheltered from the worst of the wind by the mountains. It pushed the clouds gathered up ahead at great speed to the east.

"What brings you into these mountains?" he asked casually. Seth looked back, not twitching a muscle, and then joined him.

"I said. The treasure."

"But you came so ill prepared," Barileth pointed out. "Were you not expecting it to be this far?"

Seth's eyes danced everywhere but his own. "My meat ran out weeks ago. I've been foraging what I can and I'll admit that I could have prepared more. But tell me, what reason do you have out here?"

"I come from here and go to there." Barileth took out his carving knife and a lump of bone from his pack. He settled into the carving he had started, a likeness of a dwarf fighting a giant cave spider. "Life takes me where it will."

"Ah, but the Tremble Mountains are no place for a dwarf."

"They belong to us, just as much as the goblins." Barileth tried to keep the edge out of his voice. "You must be from Guzan then, to be so ignorant."

"Not to the goblins, to my homeland. We were here ages before your kind, and we'll be the last ones here when you'r e...gone." Seth's eyes were on his knife.

"You noticed my carving?" Tension simmered beneath the surface of their waiting, and there was still an hour or more until nightfall.

Barileth held it up, let him examine it. Seth leaned closer to get a good look, exposing his neck. Barileth tightened the grip on his knife.

"Very good." Seth leaned back, then laid back on his own half-filled pack. "The likeness frightens me more than any-thing."

"It wasn't the first to fall by my blade, and it won't be the last," Barileth said.

"So you're a fighter, then. I noticed."

"Did the sword give it away?"

"For a dwarf you like to talk a lot." Seth stared at him, his cool, blue eyes devoid of any emotion. "I'd like to see you prove it."

Barileth bared his teeth. "We'll find out tomorrow, won't we?"

Seth closed his eyes, the conversation over. Before the stars came out he was snoring, or pretending to.

There was a big boulder to their right. Barileth moved his pack next to it and rolled out his blanket so that his back was to it.

By the time he was situated the sun had slipped without a hint of color behind the horizon. The clouds that had been so plentiful before were nothing but tiny strands of white, like a spider's web half destroyed.

The stars twinkled in the stillness of twilight, but Barileth couldn't get comfortable. It looked like Seth was sleeping, but he leaned back and prepared himself for a sleepless night, keeping one eye open.

He drifted in and out, keeping himself awake enough to pull the hand that held his sword, but resting enough to regain his energy. It had been a long day of hiking, they had pressed hard to get to where they were, and he needed more sleep.

When dawn finally came, and Seth yawned himself awake with a stretch of his arms, Barileth felt like he had only had an hour of rest.

"Up already?" Seth asked, noticing his open eyes. "That hit the spot, I needed a good rest."

He jumped up and squatted, then proceeded to stretch and loosen the rest of his body. Barileth shuffled his supplies away, getting enough bread out to feed himself. He wasn't going to let Seth get any more of his good provisions, if he could help it.

It didn't take long to get back on the trail, this one so overgrown and caked with dust and scrabbly bushes it made for difficult going. They either scratched his legs up if he pushed through or took too long to get around and took them too far off the path.

Still, Barileth followed Seth.

"I didn't see any of your beasts last night," Barileth said. "Don't they come out at night?"

"I said they are awake at night," Seth said. "I didn't say anything about them coming out, and we should be quiet if we don't want to rouse them."

Barileth pushed by a particularly large bush, which snapped and jabbed him. He brushed it away, a trickle of blood flowing through a small puncture.

"Up this rise," Seth said, pointing to a small ascent. He got down on his belly and started crawling up.

Barileth grumbled and crouched down, following him. Set stopped at the top, and gingerly rose his head up above the top.

"Nothing there," he whispered. "Remember, we can sneak past them easier than fighting."

"You first."

Seth took a deep breath and closed his eyes. His lips moved as if he was incanting something.

To Barileth's surprise the man glowed for a second, but when he blinked it was gone. There he was, covered in dust, nothing out of the ordinary.

And then his eyes flashed open, and Seth crawled up and over the rise.

Barileth followed, almost coughing at the dust that got in his nose. The dirt was rough and got in his mouth, so he spit it out.

Up ahead was a dark opening, a cut into the mountain that quickly went down. Other than the brush that surrounded it, nothing seemed different.

Until Barileth noticed the bones scattered around the opening. There were small animals, a bit of deer, and other larger things. It looked big enough to be a bear, but he wasn't sure.

The one thing Seth lacked was courage. He was already at the opening, head swiveling every direction.

Barileth couldn't see anything in the shadows. It was just rock that turned left and sloped down, no torches, no furniture, not even a mark on the walls.

He had the advantage when they were inside, his eyes adapting to the blackness.

⚫

The cave wasn't a warm, inviting dwarf place, but cold and sharp, with the smell of decay and death and the chill of icy water. Somewhere it dripped deep inside.

Seth had stooped, peculiarly to the left, as his head almost brushed it already, and the roof grew lower, the deeper they went. Barileth guessed that he had stopped to let his eyes adjust.

But he could see everything. Jagged stalactites, broken stalagmites, splashes of color on the wall in what could only be described as dried blood.

And a strange noise that made his hair stand on edge.

Barileth clutched his sword, bared it an inch in case he needed to use it. Seth crept forward, as quiet as a thief, and Barileth followed.

The cave narrowed and turned, but when they had only gone a few feet down the path split into three.

Seth blinked in the darkness, which had rapidly turned to black, and looked between each of them. He didn't look as sure as he once was.

And the noise was getting louder.

It was a sawing, screeching kind of noise, one that made him clench his jaw. A cold shiver ran down his spine, and he started to second guess himself.

But it was too late now, and the promise of that treasure was too powerful for him to resist. Like Seth, he supposed, he felt its pull somewhere up ahead.

Like it was calling for him.

Seth tapped him on the shoulder and motioned to the left branch. He started down it, with Barileth close on his heels.

Now the dim light from the cave opening was too far behind them to give any help, and the darkness was overpowering.

Barileth could only make out shapes, and sense the sounds getting louder. Seth shuffled ahead, ducking even lower to avoid the jagged ceiling of rock.

Even he couldn't hide the sound of his shoes on the dirt floor now, how it crunched and crackled. It made Barileth wince, for he was even louder.

I'm a dwarf, not a fairy. What was he thinking inviting me? But, alas, he had to know what was in here, and kept following.

The tunnel curved, back and forth, and went deeper. There were strange openings to the sides, filled with what could only be described as strange shapes, but the sound was loudest here.

And the air foulest.

Barileth covered his nose with his sleeve, forced to let go of his sword to get a better seal. It helped a little.

When they turned once more to the right, following the gentle arc, the darkness of the tunnel lessened.

There was a light up ahead, albeit dim. Barileth's excitement grew, the feeling in the pit of his stomach getting stronger.

What could it be? The glow of gold, or the reflections of jewels?

It grew brighter, moving and dancing, and when they were close enough, he could see why.

It was candlelight. A small flame danced on a strangely shaped squat candle, blacker than the night, that shivered and danced against the dank and cold.

Even fire, it seemed, didn't like this place, for it sputtered and spit, fighting to stay alive.

And then Barileth saw it.

Small, nondescript, but obviously a chest, it was tucked away into a corner of the cave.

He looked at Seth, who nodded. The rest of the cave was empty, lumpy rocks lining the other walls. Seth waved him forward, pointing to the chest.

Barileth took another look and gave the cave another sweeping inspection. There were no traps that he could see, nor anything up above.

So why was it that Seth hadn't gone in closer?

When Barileth looked back he was kneeling at the entrance, hands folded together and eyes closed. His mouth moved silently, but the rest of his body was as still as a statue.

Barileth sensed a change in the air. The sounds had shifted, still eerie and overpowering, but a different cadence.

But the thought of that treasure was too much to resist, and Barileth stole across the cave and passed the candle until it was within reach.

He licked his lips, sweat running down his forehead even though it was cold, and reached out to touch it.

It was made of some kind of leather, not soft, but not scratchy either, somewhere in between. About half the size of his pack, he could have picked it up and carried it, but he wanted to see what was inside first.

So, he opened it.

The hinges creaked, breaking through the strange noises around him.

"No, you fool!" Seth shouted.

Barileth jumped, and snatched up the chest, turning back in anger to yell back a snarky comment.

It died on his lips.

The shapes weren't rocks. And they weren't asleep anymore.

Seth's sword rang out of the scabbard as the strange snoring turned to roars of anger and alarm.

Blank, hollow faces of bone stared at him, jaws opening wide to reveal rows of jagged teeth.

Barileth's heart sank, and fear gripped at him. He fumbled for his own sword before realizing his hand was around the chest.

He almost dropped it, almost, but merely shifted it over to his left hand to draw his sword just in time, because the thing was upon him.

Clawed hands scratched at him. He ducked one, then slashed at the other. The thing pulled back in pain, then screeched in anger, before coming back at him.

"Run!" Seth shouted, but Barileth had no time to run. He could barely keep the claws and teeth away from him, using the chest as a shield and bashing the thing across the head.

It knocked the candle over, and they were plunged into darkness once again.

Barileth could see enough, though, and slashed its head off. It separated from the body and hit the dirt with a hollow splat, and Barileth jumped over the body and back the way they came.

Unfortunately, all the other ones were awake.

And, judging from the screams, they were angry. It echoed around him in the cave, rattled his very bones.

And it was difficult to see with no source of light.

Seth was having a harder time of it, but his movements were so fluid and light Barileth wondered how he could see so well. Evey human he had known as useless in the dark, too frail to see the noise in from t of their own face.

But he had no time to dwell on it, because another one of those beasts swiped at him. Barileth ducked and was showered with a spray of stones. A chunk of rock fell behind him, dislodged by the claw.

More were coming, too. Barileth fought and scraped, ducking and dodging. He wasn't able to stop anything, and was clipped on his helmet.

It rang through his skull, and almost turned his head sideways, but it also brought with it a clarifying anger that turned into an inferno raging through his body.

Barileth set his teeth and funneled the rage into his arms, slicing and punching where he couldn't get his sword.

Limbs were parted from their owners, faces of bone smashed with rock hard knuckles.

Pain flared down his back. Barileth turned and killed the thing that had jumped on him from behind.

He was just behind Seth now, who was leaving his own group of bodies behind him, and then they were out and into the crossroads tunnel.

Barileth took the chance to catch his breath and ask the one, burning question on his mind. "What are these things?"

"Evil," Seth replied. "Come on." He sprinted for the exit, the screeches of whatever was after them sounding through the two other tunnels they hadn't taken.

It seemed that they had kicked the hornets' nest, but Barileth had no desire to stick around and wait to see what they were.

His left leg had taken an injury, slowing him down. He didn't even remember it, but he had to sprint on it to keep up. Each step was painful, a flare of fire running up his leg.

But the way was brightening, and the smell lessening. He even felt a hint of a breeze.

Barileth looked back, then wished he hadn't. "Faster," he said through heaving breaths. He still held the chest in his left hand, but considered dropping it. It was so heavy and made such a racket it was drawing them.

I would never get my share. The thought came and passed, and he knew he wouldn't let it go no matter what was following him. Something was calling to him inside. Something that glimmered and glittered, he hoped.

And then they were at the entrance. They shot out into the light of the afternoon sun, panting and breathing.

Sweat poured down Barileth's face, and he kept going until he realized Seth had stopped.

"They don't like the light," Seth said, jerking a thumb behind him.

Faces of the monsters stared out at him, angry and screeching in high-pitched calls of pure anger. Some moved forward, but as soon as they got close to the light they hissed and backed up. Barileth counted twenty before he gave up.

"Are you sure they aren't going to follow us?"

"Oh, they will. Of that I can assure you, but only at night." Seth straightened and brushed off his shirt. The man barely had a scratch on him, and his sword was back in its scabbard.

"You fought well back there, for a dwarf."

Barileth reached up and felt the gashes in his helmet. They were deep, almost cutting through the metal, and he realized just how close to death he had come. "And you're going to tell me how you managed to see in the dark and get out without so much as a scratch."

Seth reached down and pulled up his tunic, revealing a cut that barely trickled blood from it. "It's time we made our escape." His eyes glanced to the chest still clutched in Barileth's hand.

Sheathing his own sword, Barileth took it in two hands and kept a close eye on the man as he went back the way they had come.

Shrieks and screams followed them. The sun was already on its descent, but they had a few hours to go before it would set. Long enough that Barileth started relaxing about the monsters.

His companion, however, was another story. "You still haven't answered my question."

Seth glanced back. "I've picked up a few blessing in my travels, one of which helps me see in the dark, for a short period of time."

"And in the cavern? What were you doing there?"

Seth let out a short laugh.

"What's so funny?"

"I was praying they would stay asleep." Seth wiped the corner of his eye. "I should have prayed for you to not be a fool."

Barileth frowned. "If you would have told me what we were looking for, then I wouldn't have gotten so curious, now would I?"

"When we're safely away, you'll find out what it was." Still, Barileth let Seth lead the way back to the main trail.

The air was fresh and clean, filled with the smell of the mountains that couldn't be replicated by anything else.

They stopped an hour before sunset to rest in the shade of a rocky outcropping. The chest was heavy, and Barileth was glad to get a break from carrying it.

When he got a chance to examine it, however, some of his curiosity lessened.

"It's skin..." Barileth looked closer, then pulled back his hand.

"Human skin. And others," Seth said. It was a patchwork of different colors, and Barileth decided to look too closely. "Go on, open it."

His curiosity returned, and Barileth felt its hunger. The treasure was drawing it in, but he still kept a good look on Seth out of the corner of his eye.

The man was being too casual about the whole thing, too calm. Barileth had expected him to try to take it, or at least ask for it, but nothing of the sort had happened.

With little else to do, Barileth lifted the lid.

His eyes widened, the breath caught in his throat. The subtle glow, the gentle sparkle. He shook the chest just to hear the happy tinkle, the sound he had been hearing the last few miles as they shifted.

"As promised, you get half," Seth said. Barileth glanced up at him, as cool as he could be. There wasn't a hint that they had been running from murderous monsters for the last four or five hours.

"You aren't going to try to take it all, or fool me into something worse?"

"Were you going to do the same to me?"

Barileth frowned. He had considered taking it and running off. "You're too fast."

"And from what I saw back there you're too strong. So, let's push past all this talk of betrayal and back stabbing and get to the heart of the matter." Seth's eyes flashed to him, gleaming in the failing light. "I get to choose the first half."

Their eyes locked, neither looking away. Barileth was filled with greed, and wanted it all.

But he had given his word, after all. He turned the chest and pushed it to Seth. "A deal we had, and a deal we shall honor."

Seth nodded solemnly, then dug through the chest to pull out a simple chain of gold with a gem set in a sunburst. It was the color of ruby, but glowed with a strange heat that even Barileth could tell was magical.

"Was that what you were looking for?" he asked, the beauty of it so great it took his breath away.

"Yes, it was an amulet of Torh, dedicated to luck and the sun. The man who lost it couldn't stop opining of it in his drunkenness." Seth reached down and gave it a small spin. "The last bit of luck it bestowed upon him was his life, but not enough to get this on his own."

Barileth sat back under the outcropping and watched as Seth continued his division, taking coin and gems until he had a good heap on a cloth that he rolled up and stuck in his pack. "The rest is yours."

Barileth sprang forward, snatching the chest away. There was something else in there, something deeper that had a draw more powerful than Seth's amulet.

He dug under the coins of gold and silver, past the jewels and rings and chains, until his hand came in contact with something that sent a shock wave down his arm.

His breath caught tin his throat, and his eyes went wide. Hand numb with power, Barileth pulled out a small little stone, no bigger than a caveberry.

"What is that?" Seth was next to him, and Barileth snatched the gem away from him, tucking into the deepest pocket he could find.

"Mine, a pretty thing." Barileth eyed the amulet. "I don't suppose you want to trade for that?"

As a response Seth tucked it into his tunic and went to gather some wood for a fire. Barileth took the rest of his treasure and slipped it into his secret hiding spots, some in his boots, some in secret purses, and most in his pack.

By the time Seth came back with an armful of sticks it was all gone, safely tucked away and out of sight.

But that stone in his pocked, he could still feel it tingling on his skin. What power was there, what essence?

Despite Seth's demeanor, Barileth watched him closely, seeing if he was going to try to make a move. But there was no indication of it as they got a fire going and food cooked as the sun set in the west.

"We can't keep it going for long. It will attract them," Seth said, warming his fingers by the cooking meat. They shared a meal and talked about what they might do with the treasure.

"Where will you go?" Seth asked.

Barileth scratched at his beard, then looked up into the sky. The stars twinkled in their familiar places, winking at him. He hadn't thought about it much.

"South, east, it makes no difference. I've seen nothing but the inside of a mine these last three years. I need to see the world."

"Travel to exciting places? Meet interesting people?"

"Exactly. What about you?"

"I had plans, but they changed long ago." There was a wound there that Seth didn't want to uncover, so Barileth let it slide.

"You were... useful back there," Barileth said.

Seth grinned. "So were you. I'm not sure I would have made it out alive if you hadn't killed the first few. What do you think about traveling together? I could use a good hand to watch my back."

Night had come in full now, blackness covering them like a blanket.

Barileth laughed, then put out the fire. "Why not?"

Distant screeches rode on the wind, but the two companions in the mountains settled in for the night and a well-deserved rest.

5

WHIRLING MAGERY

Istrav licked a thumb and creased it along the page, drawing it up and over, as his mouth moved along with his reading. A fat tallow candle cast an orange glow, smoking big, plump gray clouds that drifted lazily around the circular room.

Every so often he stopped and looked to the small shine on the table. It gleamed with an almost irresistible luster, red as a rose.

He coughed, choking on the smoke of the candle, which interrupted his study.

"Might be..." His big eyes blinked as he flicked a hand. The window opened, and he breathed out a small tornado of wind that swirled around the room and ruffled his brown robes. It swept the room free of smoke, and went out the window, slamming it shut with a shudder that ran through the floor.

The candle had gone out, leaving Istrav in darkness. He muttered another spell, relighting it, and stood and stretched.

His back cracked, sending a jolt of pain through his body, and he groaned. It had been hours, and still he didn't find what he was seeking.

The ruby, set into a mailed glove, distracted him. He hobbled over to it and picked it up, examining it in the faint light.

"Such as small thing. How will I ever get that much power it?" He had a habit of talking to himself, and the papers strewn about every chair but one told of why.

"Elemental enchantments failed. Capturing the power of the sun was futile, and now I'm not even sure where to begin." He rubbed his eyes, reddened with fatigue, and decided on a nice hot cup of tea.

Down the stairs he went, taking his staff along the way. He lit the tip to light his way with a word, and it clicked along the stone steps as he walked.

Out of the tower and into the main hallway he went, through the winding corridors and maze of stairs, until he entered the barrel-vaulted ceiling of the dining hall.

It was still lit up along the center row of tables with floating candelabras. A few mages were scattered throughout, but Istrav took a seat by himself.

"Tea, hot," he said to no one in particular, then settled in to brood over the glove. He had left it in his room, wanting to keep it secret, but missed having it with him to look at.

"Still working on that armor enchantment?" A pudgy mage, half his age, took a seat across from him.

"Go away Nestor, I'm in no mood to be pestered by your questions," he said, irritation heavy in his voice. He waved a hand, but it didn't dismiss the other mage.

"I find it helpful to talk through my feelings about my projects," Nestor said, painfully unaware of Istrav's discomfort. "Mayhaps you might feel unburdened to lay it on another's shoulders."

"Or I could drink my tea in peace and go back to my room." He dropped his voice and mumbled under his breath, "Still don't understand why they can't bring it up to me."

The clanging sound of armor echoed through the dining hall, near the far end of the room.

"Go on, give it a try. You've been cooped up in that room for months now trying to figure it out." Nestor's eyes crinkled as he smiled. "Couldn't hurt to get it off your chest."

Istrav went silent, hoping Nestor would get the hint. His irritation had turned into anger, tweaked by his failure. Each time Nestor brought it up twisted the blade a little deeper.

"I would be frustrated too if it took me months to finish my projects. I almost did, about this time last year." Nestor's eyebrows creased at the memory. "Fiendishly difficult translation."

Istrav looked about the room for help, but the others refused to make eye contact with him. An older mage in particular was avoiding his look, probably Nestor's first victim of the night.

The suit of armor was almost at his stable, tea splashing out the mug as it did. It came to Istrav with a horrendous rattle that shook his skull, then smashed to a halt.

Joints creaking rustily, the armor leaned forward and set the steaming mug before him.

"Thank you." Istrav looked down at the half-filled mug, wondering where the other half went, as the armor saluted with a bang on its visor, did an about face, then marched back off where it came from.

Nestor was yelling now, trying to talk over the racket, but Istrav wasn't really paying attention to him, anyway.

"--took fifteen trips to the library before I was able to get through all the scrolls." Nestor glanced into his mug. "What flavor did you get?"

"Purple," Istrav said. The taste was secondary, but the heat from the drink flowed through his stomach and out to his limbs. Reading always drained him on cold nights like these.

The wind whistled outside, coming through the dark and cold fireplace in the middle of the room. Usually filled with three or four half trees, they were dead and ash so late in the day.

Or early, depending on what time it was. Istrav had lost track of it, other than it was night.

"Nestor, I have no desire to hear your prattle any longer. I am very busy and have a lot to think about. On my own." Nestor still sat and opened his mouth to speak. "Alone," Istrav said, cutting him off. "But you can come see me another day."

Nestor's eyes brightened. "Do you mean it? I'd love to come see your room, I've never been up there--"

"Not to my room though," Istrav said curtly. *The library.* He had been by a few dozen times this week, but he hadn't checked everywhere, and Nestor's prattling had jogged his memory.

They had a big pile of ancient scrolls down there, histories or some such, but there might be something worthwhile in them.

Yes, there was almost certainly something tucked away among all those scrolls. The thought of it made him rub his hands.

And Nestor's continued talking shook him away from those thoughts.

"I'll be more than happy to bring anything you'd like. Pie, or perhaps a few sweet rolls to pass the time. I'm sure your fireplace is big enough to get a great fire going. It'll be a real pleasure to see you in your room, you'll see."

Istrav drank the rest of his tea, as hot as it was, and nodded along to try to speed the conversation. He had no intention of spending another minute with the insufferable mage.

Then, the mug was empty. "It looks like Mage Wisle might need something."

"Really? I just spent a few hours with him, but I guess--" Nestor turned to look, the old mage looking in a completely different direction, and while his head was turned Istrav sprung from his chair and made a mad dash for the exit.

When he got there, he slammed the door behind him and turned right, making a series of confusing twists and turns in the unlikely event Nestor was still trying to follow him.

The portly mage wasn't known for his speed, but then again, neither was Istrav.

His lungs and legs were on fire, cheeks puffed out as he sucked in air. He leaned against a column, catching his breath in the cold alcove, and kept to the darkness.

His eyes darted around the corridor, examining a long hallway that he hadn't been in in ages. A twinkling of a memory disturbed him.

"This is the..." But could it be? He hadn't been down here since he was a novice, green around the thumb and wet behind the ears.

But...

Istrav sniffed. There it was, that scent that was bringing back familiar days of scrubbing and washing, the faint smell of lye.

It must have been closer to the laundry than he thought, and he had an urge to go see if his memory was betraying him.

He put the problem behind him, thinking it might be a good way of getting his mind off of it. He had been dwelling on it for a few weeks, and it was starting to get locked inside his mind. Maybe he did need to let it air out.

Or maybe he needed to wash it away.

Either way, he took one last look to make sure the coast was clear, and proceeded down the corridor.

The hours he had spent here, the friends he had made. Constant hours of conversation flooded back to him. With little else to do, the other novices and him did nothing but talk and wash.

A few more familiar turns and there it was, the great oaken door half hanging off its hinges like always, a few dents and bruises added since his time.

He knelt, peering down, and put a finger in the over-sized dent he had made with an old cast iron pot.

He pushed it open, walking into his past and another world.

But the old room was quiet and dark, still strewn with the remnants of dish-washing and laundry, but not a soul in sight.

Istrav looked around, remembering things as they once were, and not as they appeared. He was surprised to remember those times so fondly. When he was living through them it was a nightmare of chores and corporeal punishment.

Nothing was ever good enough for old Rastna, the head cook and slave-driver of the novices. Even though they could get the pots and pans to clean themselves, he absolutely forbade it and had it codified with the Archmage.

The light and memories faded, replaced with the cobwebs and dust a half inch thick. His few steps into the room had disturbed it, and knocked it up to tickle his nose.

He held back a sneeze, then turned and left, pausing one last time to see it.

Armor, pots and pans.

Something about the memories lodged in his brain, and he couldn't shake it off. Istrav shook his head to clear it and shut the door.

He went down to the library, that nagging feeling following him through the twists and turns and columned hallways of the magery.

When he walked through the two massive, bronze doors of the library he felt more at ease. Here, surrounded by books and tomes and scrolls of every shape and size, he was even more at home than his own room of many years. And in this, he was not alone.

Mages sat at desks and in corners overflowing with paper, leafing through them in their own small quests.

Their presence reminded him of his own reason for coming here, putting to rest the strange feeling around his shoulders, and his focus returned.

Istrav walked past all the others, down the leaning bookshelves and the sputtering candles that had melted a thousand times until they were overrun with wax.

At the back of the room a small circular stairway led down to the lower reaches of the library, and he followed it. Not the first left, or the second, or even the third. There were still mages at study in those levels, but he walked, boots clicking along the stone, until he finally reached the tenth level below the library.

The stairs ended in the earth, remnants of the last time it had been excavated to house more knowledge. Down here there weren't well apportioned bookshelves graced with carvings, or statues of old mages and ancient writings, but it was where the overflow of the things less used had come.

Beaten up scrolls and ill-used books graced its simple, unadorned shelves hastily assembled. Istrav walked carefully, avoiding protruding nails and bent, sharp slivers, until he arrived in the middle of the room.

When he looked around, he wasn't sure where to start. There was no semblance of order, nor had the librarians gotten around to cataloging them all, but he noticed a relatively fresh box on the floor and shrugged. It was as good a place as any.

So he went to it, picking out the least worn scrolls. One had an oily feel to it, and looked promising, but turned out to be an account of sheep written in a scrawling hand that never seemed to stop.

He didn't have much luck with the next one, or the one after, and soon had run through the whole box.

Istrav stood and blinked, then went to the next shelf. On it he found various accounts, but nothing useful.

It went on this way for hours, until he finally couldn't take the exhaustion and crawled back upstairs to his own bed.

It was night again when he awoke, and after a quick breakfast of orange pudding and spicy meat he returned.

About midday he happened upon an account of a silver-smith that looked promising. He was working enchanted jewels into his rings, but never wrote how he got them or how they were made.

It was a great disappointment, but Istrav set it aside, nonetheless. In his disappointment he conjured up a wind, shaking free everything in the room, to put them back onto the shelves by height.

Istrav marched at random through the bookshelves, stopping at one on a whim and turning. There was a small scroll caught between two bigger ones.

"You shouldn't have been able to escape my magic," Istrav muttered. He plucked it out. It was soft and buttery feeling, and smelled nice. Not like a perfume, but compared to the musty and molded scrolls around him, it was a pleasant refreshment.

He turned it around in his hand, surprised to find a red seal on it. The symbol on it was nothing he had ever seen, a rose etched on the face of a circular shape.

He put his thumb to the edge of it, a thrill running through him. Who knew what was inside, what secret knowledge it held?

He was alone in the room, and made sure. For a moment he considered taking it to his room and opening there in the safety of his wards, but his curiosity got the better of him.

With one sharp snap he broke the seal.

It seemed to echo in the empty room, a small whine rising then dying away just as quickly. He unrolled the small scrap of parchment, holding his breath.

There wasn't much on it, and nothing he could understand. There were a few scratches at the top, then a strange set of symbols underneath.

Istrav's heart beat faster. His palms started sweating, and he rolled it up quickly and shoved it into his sleeve.

The room was still empty, but the sudden urge to hide it overcame him. Istrav scrambled to the stairs and up them, hunching over past the others in the library to avoid any hint of eye contact, and then up to his room.

His feet were aching by the time he arrived and slammed his door behind him. He was breathing heavily, and his hand went to the scroll. His fingers clasped around it, and he breathed a sigh of relief. *Still there.*

His room was empty, as it always was, but his entrance dislodged a paper on the chair and it floated to the ground.

Istrav picked it up and put it back in its proper place, on a disheveled stack on the chair, and took his prize to his desk.

Sweeping aside other assorted writings and odds and ends, he cleared a space for it.

For the next few hours he poured over it, scrutinized it and tried to wrack his brain on where, if anywhere, he had seen that writing. He went back to his old notes, and every book on languages he had, which, granted, wasn't many, until he was too exhausted to stay awake any longer and dropped onto his bed and into a dreamless sleep.

When he awoke the next night, for it was now dark outside his window, he sprang right back to work. Despite more frustrating hours, he came up empty-handed.

He took a trip to the library, getting every book of ancient languages he could think of, and pored over them for the next few weeks.

They were of little use, however, and the text on the scroll proved impossible to decipher.

Weeks passed, his beard grew, and the scroll continued to frustrate him. Each time he thought he was making progress, it unraveled before his eyes.

Countless trips back and forth to the library, and a few close calls avoiding Nestor, didn't help much.

He was at his wit's end.

Everywhere he went he thought about it, obsessed over it. It was in his mind constantly.

And every day he went without finding out what it meant was one more day closer to insanity.

Istrav walked his room one night, trying not to look at it. He could draw the rune in his mind, and in his sleep, he had drawn it so many times.

In fact, he had almost taken to drawing it on every surface of his room, but something held him back. This was no trifle to play with, but a long-forgotten secret.

Who knew what power it hid?

"But I will find out," he muttered to himself. His fingers wrung, and his breathing was heavy. He made circles around the table.

There wasn't much else to do, every road led to a dead end. A tickle of advice somewhere in the back of his mind made him stop pacing.

"No, I can't do it." But what else was there to do? He had gotten nowhere on his own. Wind rattled at the windows, drawing his attention to the lightening horizon.

The sun was coming up, and that meant breakfast was going to be served.

If there was one place to find him, a mealtime was it. Everyone knew it.

But he wasn't ready, and caught himself chewing his fingernails, an old habit he had dropped years ago, or thought he had.

"Just a conversation, nothing more. A few words. It couldn't hurt." He was longing for human interaction, in a daze he realized how long it had been since he talked to one.

Istrav took his most precious possessions, the scroll and the glove, and set them into his secret box.

He turned his golden key and slipped it back around his neck before setting the box under the floorboard in the corner and whispering a few words over it.

It faded from view, and he touched it to make sure it was still there.

The warm wood underneath his fingers, despite his eyes telling him it was empty, reassured him.

The dining hall was just beginning to fill as he entered, mages streaming from every corner of the magery and conversation following like water over a riverbed.

He picked out his voice at once, distinct in the chatter that echoed off the great vaulted ceiling.

A fire was raging in the great fireplace, spreading heat and light that somehow made Istrav feel better.

Everyone else was trying to avoid him, and Istrav pretended to do the same at first, but he took a seat within close proximity and made eye contact.

"Istrav, I haven't seen you down here in a while. Working on something exciting?" His rose-colored jowls jiggled as he talked.

"Perhaps."

That was all the invitation Nestor needed, and he took a seat directly across from him.

"Tell me everything about it. Are you writing a new tome, or translating something? Ah, that's it!" Nestor broke out into a huge smile. "You need help with a translation, don't you?"

"No," Istrav said sharply, beginning to wonder if this wasn't a good idea after all. He soothed his tone. "No, I don't need help, but..." Nestor waited with bated breath. "I could use a good nudge in the right direction."

"Say no more! I'll have you know that some of the best guides are here in the library."

"I've tried those," Istrav said, cutting him off. "They haven't worked well enough."

"Really?" Nestor's eyebrows descended, coming together in a big knot. "Did you try *Ancient Languages*?" Istrav nodded. "*Ecumenical Sayings*? *Translations in Runes*? All the ancient scrolls of Salabinth?"

"Even those."

"Well, you have got yourself into a tight corner." Nestor blew out a great gust of air, cheeks puffed out like a chipmunk. "I'd like to see what you've got." He looked hopeful, but Istrav kept a stone face.

"Eggs and ham, with a side of bacon," Istrav said. Nestor ordered his three plates of pancakes with extra butter, and then launched into a diatribe on the many ways to translate, from ancient to the modern.

Istrav tried to look bored, but Nestor was making sense for once, none of his precious chitchat and prattle about things that didn't matter.

It helped that Istrav was keenly interested in this topic at that very moment.

The food came out, dozens of suits of armor clamping and tramping with such a racket that it made his ears tremble. Nestor kept talking all through it, raising his voice to an almost yell to be heard.

"No need to be so loud," Istrav said, clapping his hands over his ears. "Just wait until they're gone."

Thankfully, he did, although Istrav could see the pained look on his face of what Nestor was holding back.

"Have you tried reading it backward?" Nestor asked. "Sometimes I like to go up to down and backwards to see if it will shake anything loose. I like to think of it as a tree, and when I go upside down—I'm a monkey." He laughed, although Istrav didn't see the humor in it.

But the comment had him thinking. "That might do the trick." Maybe not backwards, but what if he had the scroll upside down this whole time?

Istrav stood, cutting off Nestor in mid-sentence. "Where are you going?" he asked as Istrav turned.

"Back to the library," he said over his shoulder, going that direction and fast enough that Nestor wouldn't follow.

He wasn't sure why he had lied. It didn't feel right, but he turned around the corner and went back to his room the long way.

When he got there, he shut and locked his door, and turned back to the hiding spot. The chest was still there, and he restored it to the visible realm and took out the two items. One was cool to the touch, the other warm, and he set them on the table to study.

The scroll he unrolled and turned upside down. He had spent all this time staring at it he had it memorized.

All the ancient languages he had pored over, spent countless hours trying to decipher, but what if they weren't a language at all, but all of them were figures of power?

Something Nestor said jogged a memory, an idea.

But he wasn't sure it was the right thing to do. Who knew what these runes were for, or what power they held?

Or if they held any power at all. Istrav walked around the room, pacing out a path through the clutter and mess. It had been months since he had touched any of it, and the stacks and piles had grown even larger than normal. Now there was no place for him to sit and think other than his bed.

Which he did, knocking over a pile of books perched at the foot of it.

"Confound it." He pushed them out of the way, not bothering to pick anything up or put it in any semblance of order, and then sat back.

He stared at the mailed glove for a long time, longer than he knew what to do with.

His heart was beating at the thrill of what he was about to do, but his fear was so much larger. It was a battle inside of him, and a voice of caution near the back of his head.

But he had spent so much time on this, it would be a shame to lose it.

Or worse, have to share with a mid-wit like Nestor.

The thought was a sliver in his mind, getting into it and burrowing like a worm, until it had consumed the fear and grew fat on his anticipation.

Istrav went to his desk and got out his most precious inks. He plucked a few hairs from his head and tied them together, attaching them to a stick with a word, and set about his task.

Each stroke he made with an almost fervored madness. Each stroke was thin, a light trace that built up the runes. Each stroke made him more and more sure of his actions.

He drew each of the runes in a circle on the gem, saving the largest for the center.

This one took the bulk of his attention. Each stroke was light, but firm. It took him over an hour before he was finished.

And when he was, he leaned back and wiped the sweat off his forehead, breathing a sigh of relief. He was exhausted, like he had just been running all day, and he could feel it in his bones.

But something else was happening, and it took all of his attention.

The gem was...changing. He breathed a hint of power into it, and the rune glowed golden in a burst of light.

Istrav covered his eyes, but he could still feel the power through his hand.

And he sensed a growing feeling as the light died down enough for him to look at it again without it blinding him.

The runes were there, but they pulsed with energy. It crackled through the air, made his hair stand on end, and he tasted it.

His heart was beating faster than it ever had now.

It called to him, pulled at him.

Istrav couldn't resist. He reached out to touch it.

Then blinked.

Something closed around his wrist. It was heavy, but warm, and pulsating.

The glove was on his hand. It looked as if it were made for it, and he wondered how it had happened.

He admired it, lifted it up to the glow of the candlelight. The gem shimmered, catching his eye.

The runes were fading now. He wasn't sure why, or what it meant.

Then something rippled on the other side of the table.

A hole opened, or what looked like a hole, as black as night and thicker than ink.

Istrav's hand was pulled to it, guided by the glove. He tried to pull it off, but it was like it had been attached to his skin.

No matter how much he pulled and prodded, it wouldn't budge.

And it was humming, growing more attracted to the hole that was his size now, but still growing.

Istrav panicked, tried every spell of releasing he could think of, but his words trickled out into stammering.

The gem was heating up, burning his arm now, and was inches away from the surface of whatever that hole was made of.

And it was larger than him now.

With horror, he realized it was going to go into it. The first fingers touched the surface, rippled it, then slipped inside.

And before Istrav could stop it, he was pulled inside.

The hole snapped shut, winking out of existence. The fire fluttered, and the candles flickered in the empty room as the scroll ignited and burned to ash.

ECLECTIC STORIES

Thank you for spending your precious time reading this book.

If stories make you salivate, learn more about lore, take an exclusive sneak peek behind the scenes, and get writing updates in my newsletter, Eric's Eclectic Stories.

As a bonus you'll get *Stories from the Deep*, a Patmos Sea Fantasy Adventure anthology that gives a glimpses of lore, extra prologues and epilogues, and character backstories.

If you aren't satisfied, unsubscribe at any time.

Join at erickercher.com.

-Eric Kercher

ALSO BY ERIC KERCHER

Patmos Sea Fantasy Adventure Series

Fathomless Pursuit
Architect's Prize
Ironbound Path
Sunken Prey
Unanswered Prophecy
Hardened Pilgrim
Final Peace

Seventh Hall Chronicles

Seventh Hall
Ode to the Survivors
Bastion of the Deep

Epic of Hornblood Castle

Siege of the Unfinished Keep
Winter at Hornblood
Branch of the Everlong

Anthologies

Red Eagle Anthology
Searchlight Anthology

About Author

Eric Kercher was born and raised in a small town on the Great Plains on good books. After attending a small state school on the east coast he joined the US Navy to serve his country and explore the world. He worked on submarines, and the world beneath the waves captivated him with all its mysteries and wonders. After spending time in larger cities, he's settled down in a quiet town with his wife and children. When not on an adventure in a good book the author enjoys creating dust woodworking, architecture, and spending time with loved ones.

Find out more at www.erickercher.com.

www.ingramcontent.com/pod-product-compliance
Lightning Source LLC
Chambersburg PA
CBHW030943310726
48969CB00008B/2361